Always laugh
RS Grey

THE
ALLURE OF
Dean Harper

USA TODAY BESTSELLING AUTHOR
R.S. GREY

Published: R.S. Grey 2015
authorrsgrey@gmail.com
Editing: Editing by C. Marie
Cover Design: R.S. Grey
Stock Photos courtesy of Shutterstock ®
All rights reserved.
ISBN: 1517265347
ISBN-13: 978-1517265342

CHAPTER ONE

LILY

I PRIDE MYSELF on knowing a good bartender when I see one. Unfortunately, the guy across the bar from me wasn't one. I'd already watched him botch his last three drink orders. A tad too orange juice here, not enough gin there. The customers took the glasses with big smiles and even bigger tips, but I knew better. It was my job to know the difference between a decent drink and a cocktail that earned its keep at a place like this.

Well, technically "job" incorrectly implies that I was being paid.

"Are you going to order something or…"

The waitress purposely let her sentence trail off, but I heard the message loud and clear: *"Or just sit on that bar stool for another hour, staring at the menu like a freak."*

I turned over my shoulder and flashed her an apologetic smile. "I'll probably just need another minute to decide."

She huffed out an annoyed breath and flipped her notepad closed. I tried to offer an apology, but she was already gone, waltzing toward a table full of red-faced businessmen with cash to burn. They were already on their fourth round of drinks for the night. One of them reached out to grip the back of her leg as he ordered. I rolled my eyes and turned back to my happy hour menu.

I'd practically memorized it, but I was no closer to deciding what I was going to order. It was my first night in New York and I was out alone, a little broke, and a lot hungry. I'd convinced myself that I could splurge for my first night in the city, but the twenty-something dollar appetizers still made me gasp. What choice did I have though? Food critics critique food. Good food. They don't rank the top ten fast food joints in order of least-likely-to-give-you-a-heart-attack-on-the-spot. If I wanted to transcend Buzzfeed and actually create a name for myself in the city, I had to rub elbows at the best restaurants. I just hadn't quite worked out how I would afford it yet.

The couple to my right were served another round of appetizers: seared mahi mahi and fresh spring rolls. I watched them dive in, not even bothering with the Thai basil dipping sauce. *Heathens.*

"Can I buy you a drink?"

I shifted my gaze from my neighbors over to the balding gentleman sliding into the bar stool beside me. He looked closer to my dad's age than my own, but that didn't stop him from eyeing me like I was the answer to all of his prayers. Little did he know, he was about to be the answer to mine.

I smirked and dropped my menu onto the bar. "How about the crunchy tuna rolls instead?"

His smile fell. "Are you serious?"

Why is it customary for men to buy women drinks when they want to get in their pants? You know what will drop my pants? *Crunchy tuna rolls*.

"This restaurant is known for their food, not for their drinks," I explained.

His gaze slid from my face down to the menu and back again.

"But, I was kidding," I added to ease his mind. I may have been from Texas, but even there, gifts from strangers seldom came without strings attached. I was desperate, not stupid.

Still, he ignored my protest and flagged down a passing waitress to put in the order.

I should have felt guilty for asking him to order me food when I had zero intentions of going home with him, but I didn't. After I took a picture of the food for my blog, I'd let him eat it. As soon as the crunchy tempura and spicy aioli hit his mouth, he'd be thanking me for suggesting it.

He dragged his gaze down my body and I narrowed my eyes on him. He was wider than he was tall, with a pinstripe suit and sweat coating his forehead. I watched him dab away at it with a handkerchief before he spoke up.

"So are you from around here?" he asked.

"Nope. You?"

I didn't want to lead him on, but until I had a photo of that crunchy tuna roll saved on my phone, I had to humor him with conversation.

"Staten Island, born and raised," he bragged. "I do construction in the city though."

I nodded as I pulled out my phone. It was rude to check it during conversation, but I couldn't resist. I'd put in an application at a restaurant earlier that day and was anxious to hear back from them. I doubted they'd get in touch with me during happy hour on a Friday night, but I still had to check.

He scooted his stool almost imperceptibly closer to mine, dropped his hand to my leg, and squeezed.

"Know anythin' bout construction, honey?" he asked with a thick New York accent.

My heart stopped as I registered the feeling of his meaty paw on my bare skin. It was there for one, maybe two seconds before I reached down and yanked it off.

"Touch me again and I'll stab you in the eyes with these chopsticks."

His beady little eyes opened wide at my threat—clearly, he wasn't used to his prey biting back.

I was already scooting off my barstool when my phone vibrated in my hand. *What a perfect exit.* I wanted to get far away from Meaty McGrabsALot *and* I had to answer my phone.

He twisted on his stool and threw his hands up in defeat as I walked away. "Oh c'mon. Stay! I was just playin' around."

"Well then, you should work on your delivery, 'cause that wasn't very *playful*."

By the time I pushed through the door of the restaurant, I didn't have time to consider the unknown number on my phone. It was about to stop ringing and I hated returning calls from strange numbers. That inevitable conversation: *"Yes, hi, you just called me—No, I don't know anyone named Lupita—uh, no soy Lupita, lo siento."* Apparently, I shared my digits with an elderly woman from the Dominican Republic. Whodathought?

"Hello? Can you hear me?" I answered as I held the phone to my ear.

The city noise made it nearly impossible to hear the

woman on the other end of the line. I squatted down, wedged my finger into my free ear, and pressed the phone against the other as hard as possible. If I'd shoved it any closer, I'd probably have radiated my brain.

"Hello—can you hear me?" I asked again.

"Yes. Hey. Is this Lily Black?"

I covered my ear and ducked back against the building, hoping it would help block the noise.

"Yes. Who's this?"

"Zoe. From Provisions."

My heart leapt at the name of the restaurant I'd been waiting to hear back from.

"Listen, I know this is kind of insane of me to ask, but we're really short staffed tonight." Her voice cut off and then I heard muffled yells from her end of the phone. A second later, she spoke back through the receiver. "Lily, you still there?"

I smiled. "Yes."

"Is there any way you could get here like…" She paused again. "Now?"

I stared at the street signs around me like that would help. *Ha.* I'd spent twelve hours in New York. The only street names I knew were Broadway, 5th, and Wall Street—none of which would help me in this situation, but I didn't want to let Zoe know that. *You can get anywhere in the city fairly quickly right? It's an island; how big can it possibly be?*

"Uh, I think I can be there in like ten minutes, but I haven't had an interview or anything."

She laughed into the phone like I'd just told the funniest joke she'd ever heard.

"Where do you see yourself in ten years?"

"I…uhh…"

"God, that was a joke. Get here."

The line went dead and I stared down at the black screen in shock. I had ten minutes. *Well, now nine minutes and fifty seconds. SHIT.* I typed Provisions into Google Maps and then cringed as the route popped up. By car, I could get there in eight minutes. Walking, I'd need at least twenty. I didn't have cash to spare on a cab, and I wasn't brave enough to try the subway system. That left me with one option. I tied my long hair up in a ponytail, threw my purse over my shoulder, and took off in a dead sprint toward Provisions.

By the time I arrived outside, sweat dripped from my brow, I'd skinned a knee after tripping over a curb, and I was pretty sure I had about five different pieces of gum stuck to the bottom of my heels. All in all, it wasn't my best look.

Clumps of people crowded outside the restaurant, waiting to be seated. I edged my way through them, trying to catch my breath as I went. Finally, I arrived in front of a massive black door flanked by two round topiaries. Right above the door, shining under a spotlight, "Provisions" was spelled out in thin metal letters.

I reached for the door handle, still breathing like a wild woman as I stepped into the dim light of the restaurant's foyer. Untreated marble floors sat below crisp grey walls. Black-and-white photos were positioned at eye level around the small room. They were snapshots of everyday objects: an apple, an iris, stacked bricks; it was the scale and simplicity of the photos that turned them into something intriguing.

"Uhh, can I help you with something?"

I turned toward the hostess positioned behind a black podium. A gold desk lamp shined down on her list of chosen people who'd get to dine in the restaurant that night. Her sour expression told me I clearly wasn't one of them.

"I'm here to see Zoe," I explained, trying to keep the exhaustion out of my voice.

The woman arched a brow at me, scanning down my body once before returning her sharp stare to my eyes. I knew without the aid of a mirror that I looked frazzled. Most of my blonde hair had fallen out of my ponytail and there was definitely blood running down my shin. Still, her sourpuss stare didn't affect me. I could see right through her fake tan and eyelash extensions. Her smoky eye shadow was caked on so thick I was surprised she could even manage to lift her eyelids. Women like her didn't faze me. Why? Because they were predictable, almost like they were playing a part they'd seen on daytime TV.

I held my ground and crossed my arms. The message was clear: *your move.*

I would have stayed like that until she went to retrieve Zoe, but luck was on my side. A moment later, a brunette woman with a short pixie cut rounded the corner into the foyer like she was on a mission. She glanced from the hostess to me, and then back again.

"Crystal, what the hell are you doing? We don't pay you to stand there with resting bitch face."

I resisted the urge to laugh.

Crystal rolled her eyes, but held her tongue. I watched her grab a clipboard off the podium and huff away in a cloud of perfume and glitter.

When she was out of earshot, the pixie-cut woman turned her attention to me.

"Please tell me you aren't Lily."

My confidence faltered.

"Zoe?" I asked, wiping my sweaty palm on the side of

my dress.

She ran her hand down her cheek.

"No. No. This won't work out," she said, shaking her head.

"What? Why?" She hadn't even given me five minutes to prove myself.

She glared at me, waving her hand out in front of her. "Because the last thing we need in this restaurant is another fucking Barbie doll."

CHAPTER TWO

LILY

I KNEW THAT Zoe saw when she looked at me. I could sense her disdain. Within five seconds of meeting me, she'd already lumped me in with the Crystals of the world. *How wrong she was.*

She crossed her toned arms and I scanned over the colorful tattoos running from her shoulders to her elbows.

"Give me a chance to prove myself," I said, holding my ground.

She pursed her lips. "Listen, you're not the first girl to come in here with a face that could kill, though yours looks like the first pair of natural lips I've seen in a decade. What's your angle? You want to be an actress? Model? You want to find yourself a sugar daddy to fund your stay in the city?"

I let her barbs glance off and narrowed my eyes on her. It made sense, really. Zoe's job was to manage a wait staff made up of self-absorbed sociopaths. Why would she want to add one more to the mix? Lucky for her, I wasn't a sociopath, and I was only somewhat self-absorbed.

"Where's your bar?" I asked, ignoring her line of questioning.

She tilted her head, confused.

Fine. I didn't need her help. I could already glimpse the main bar in the restaurant, tucked against the sidewall. There were two guys working behind it, moving like cyclones trying to fill orders as fast as possible. The setup would be simple—bars aren't rocket science. After I'd finished up culinary school and a two-semester bartending program, I'd landed a job working at a dive bar one town over from mine. No big deal, right? Wrong. New York yuppies had nothing on a bunch of burly Texans. They wanted their drinks, and they wanted them yesterday.

I moved past Zoe without another word and bee-lined for the bar. It was hard to navigate through the crowd, especially as they clumped together, trying to get the bartender's attention. I pushed through them, using elbows and sheer force when needed.

The bar came up to my stomach and there wasn't an entrance in sight, but I didn't let that stop me. I tossed my purse over onto the ground and then pushed myself up onto the black marble countertop.

"What are you doing?" one of the bartenders yelled as I swung my legs over the bar.

"Finishing up my job interview," I threw back, not bothering with any more explanation. My feet landed with a thud on the black rubber mat and then I turned back to the crowd. Half a dozen people were staring back at me with shocked expressions. I let them gather their wits as I washed my hands and reached for a spare drink shaker.

The other bartender waltzed over, his male-model looks completely wasted on me. I had a thing about guys who spent more time in the powder room than I did.

"You can't be back here," he said, trying to reach for the drink shaker in my hand.

I pulled it out of his grasp and smiled.

"I'm here on special order from Zoe," I lied, only somewhat.

His mouth dropped and I turned back to the crowd, bored with him already.

"You." I pointed at the petite girl in front of me. She had a fifty-dollar bill tucked in her hand and was being crushed by the crowd pushing in behind her. "What are you drinking?"

She stared back and forth between me and the other bartender, unsure of whether she was allowed to answer me.

The bartender threw his hands up and walked away. "I don't get paid enough for this shit."

I smirked as I stared at the girl, waiting for her to reply.

"Uh, okay. I need two dirty martinis and a gin fizz," she stammered.

Easy.

"Do you prefer a certain type of gin?"

I bent down to check out the liquor offering behind the bar. They had a few good brands of dry gin, but I preferred the cucumber and rose flavor that Hendrick's offered. I set out three cocktail glasses and got to work on the dirty martinis. Ice, gin, brine from cocktail olives, and extra dry vermouth were added to the shaker before I tossed it all together and strained the mixture into the first two cocktail glasses. I rinsed the shaker and reached for lemons, but stopped short when I couldn't find any gimme syrup. I decided I'd have to bring in supplies for my next shift if I lasted through the night.

Instead of bothering Captain America and Ken doll, I found simple syrup and hoped it would do. I didn't have time to ask where every single ingredient was if I wanted to actually help the other bartenders work through the crowd.

I directed the woman to pay with the other bartender and focused my attention on the next customer. Though he probably hated it, one of the bartenders, Brian, and I worked out a system within five minutes. I took orders, and filled them, and he cashed out the customers or transferred their drinks to the tab at their table.

I'd finished making two White Russians, a Sea Breeze, a screwdriver, two more dirty martinis, and a slew of gin and tonics before Zoe joined me behind the bar and gripped my arm. I set down my shaker and turned my attention to her.

"I get it. Barbie knows her shit," she said, pulling me away from my self-assigned station. "Brian keep up the bar. Lily will be back in a few minutes."

I smiled and let her pull me away. If I was coming back, that meant I'd landed the job.

I followed Zoe through the restaurant, taking in the scenery as we went. Provisions continued to surprise me. The floor plan was spectacular, but the open courtyard in the center of the restaurant took my breath away. I hadn't seen anything like it before. Customers were crowded around tables, eating under a grove of trees. Twinkle lights hung from the branches, basking them all in gentle light.

We circled around the perimeter of the courtyard and then Zoe led me into a back hallway toward a door that read "Employees only."

We stepped through the door and the restaurant's quiet

music was replaced with silence. Our shoes echoed through the hall and I reached out to stop her so I could plead my case.

"Honestly, you don't have to worry about my intentions with this job." She turned to face me. "I'm here because I need a job in New York. I'd prefer bartending to serving, but I'm flexible. I have a culinary degree and I've completed bartending school. I've worked just about every server job imaginable, so if there's anyone qualified to work here, it's me."

She angled her head and studied me.

"Sounds like you could be doing something a little more impressive than waiting tables."

I shrugged. She wasn't telling me anything I hadn't already considered myself.

"I want to work in the restaurant industry, but until I find my niche, I just need to get my bills paid."

"What about managing?"

I grimaced. "No offense, but it's not my cup of tea."

She laughed. "Fair enough. Usually I have to get Dean to sign off on all new hires, but he's out of town and I need you at the bar tonight."

My back straightened at the mention of his name. He was the whole reason I'd applied at Provisions in the first place.

"My best friend is actually dating Dean's friend, Julian. That's how I knew you were hiring."

Zoe nodded. "Is that so? So you've met Dean before?"

I swallowed. Would it be a deal breaker if I hadn't?

"No, but I've been told we'll get along just fine."

My throat tightened over the lie. When my best friend Josephine had first told me about Dean and his restaurants, her exact words were something like "you and Dean will get along like oil and water", but what did it matter? He would be my boss's boss's boss. We didn't really *have* to get along.

I followed Zoe through the back offices until we pushed into what looked like an employee locker room. A row of stalls lined one wall, with sinks directly across from them. Black lockers lay half unused along the right-hand side, with clothes and backpacks spilling out of them.

"Here, this should fit," Zoe said, pulling out a dark purple garment from a Tupperware bin above the lockers.

I unrolled the piece of fabric and then glanced up at her over the top of it.

"You have got to be kidding me. Is this actually considered clothing?"

She smirked.

"Consider it a 'Welcome to Provisions' gift courtesy of Dean Harper."

CHAPTER THREE

DEAN

"WHERE TO MR. HARPER?"

The answer should have been one word: home. I'd been traveling for the last nine hours and my bed was calling my name. Unfortunately, my day was far from over. It'd been nearly a week since I'd stepped foot inside my newest restaurant and my control tendencies were starting to flare up.

I never liked leaving a fledging restaurant for very long. Management and staff needed a few weeks of babysitting before I felt like the machine was sufficiently oiled. My team at Provisions had undoubtedly taken advantage of my absence.

I met the driver's eyes in the rearview mirror. "Provisions. Up on—"

"I know where it is, sir."

I nodded and turned my gaze out the window, trying to force my focus from my trip back to work. The fact that my suit stunk slightly of farm animals made the task nearly impossible.

Heading to Iowa to visit my family's farm had been long overdue and highly unnecessary. The first day, my parents put on fake smiles, but soon enough questions and opinions were flying worse than the horse flies.

"You're thirty-three years old, Dean. When are you going settle down? Start a family?"

Uh, never. Is that too soon? How about never plus infinity?

"You think that fast 'n' hard life will sustain you for long?"

What do they think I'm doing in New York? Crack? I work twelve hours a day.

"Seems awfully lonely…"

No. Just last week Kelly, Carmella, and Svetlana kept me plenty occupied.

My parents couldn't wrap their heads around how I could possibly be happy as a restaurateur in New York. They'd married at eighteen, had me at twenty. Their lives revolved around farm life and family life. Needless to say, I'd wanted something very different.

And I had it.

I was the top restaurateur in New York City. In the last few years, I'd had my hand in opening eleven restaurants around the city. This year, I planned on doubling that number.

"Here we are, Mr. Harper," my driver said from the front seat. "Should I wait here until you're done?"

I slid a generous tip over the console and shook my head. I had no way of knowing the current state of the restaurant. Likely, I'd be in there for hours. "I'll call a cab. You can take my luggage back to my house and then head home yourself."

He pocketed the tip with a wide smile. "Of course, sir."

I nodded and slipped out of the back of the town car, buttoning my black jacket as I stood. My gaze slid over the facade of the building. The ivy was growing nicely along the exterior wall. The spotlight over the door perfectly illuminated the restaurant's name, just as I'd intended. Even at ten o'clock, there were clumps of people milling out on the sidewalk.

I pushed through the crowd and stepped into the restaurant, bracing myself for the worst. I'd put my most seasoned employee in charge, but even Zoe was bound to have problems without my help for a week. A quick scan of the foyer indicated that the place was still as I'd left it, though one of the picture frames was slightly ajar, but I couldn't really blame Zoe for that. Could I? *No.* Even I had my limits.

"Mr. Harper! You're back!"

I snapped my attention to the hostess, who was staring at me with giant doe eyes from behind the podium. She filled out the Provisions uniform well and was maintaining the kind of look that the clientele of my restaurants expected. "We weren't expecting to see you tonight."

I shrugged. "Shouldn't be a problem. Every night should run as if I'm present."

She giggled, though I definitely hadn't told a joke. "Of course. Speaking of presents, let me unwrap this one for you."

She rushed forward around the podium, reaching for my jacket. The movement caused the bottom of her dress to flare up, but I wasn't fazed. When I was in work mode, my employees were numbers to me. Nameless, faceless parts of my machine. I needed them to arrive on time, smile at customers, and clean up their assigned tables before clocking out every night. That's it.

Her finger brushed the edge of my collar and I held up my hand to stop her.

"It's fine. Where's Zoe?"

Her bottom lip jutted out and her arm fell limp back to her side. "Back in the offices. I think she's been trying to catch up on paperwork ever since she hired that new girl."

My back stiffened. "New girl?"

There was a policy in place in every single one of my restaurants: I had the final say for all new hires. I had good instincts and I liked to look every employee in the eye at least once before they represented my company. Zoe knew that rule, and for the first time, she'd chosen to ignore it.

The hostess' frown deepened. "Yeah, she came in earlier looking *totally* homeless. I can't believe Zoe actually hired her. I thought she was going to kick her to the curb—"

"Thank you," I interrupted. "But it's none of your concern who we choose to hire."

I hated when employees acted chummy with me. I wasn't some friend from book club. I was her boss and so was Zoe.

I wanted to tell her off for trying to throw Zoe under the bus, but excited shouts rang out from one of the restaurant's bars, drawing my attention. I stepped forward and narrowed my eyes, curious about the commotion.

The four bars lining the interior courtyard of Provisions had been packed ever since opening night, but I'd yet to see a circus-like crowd form around any of them.

Why is one forming now?

I caught short snippets of conversations as I made my way closer to the bar.

"Am I toasted or was she really hot?"

"Dude. I bought four drinks. FOUR. Why?"

"You looked into her eyes. You shouldn't have done it, man."

"She's a wizard!"

I smirked. It wasn't the first time one of my employees had spurred devotion from customers. *That's why I hire beautiful people*. During the interview process, my team and I vetted the applicants based on their looks and their experience—in that order. No customer gives a shit if his prime rib comes out a little late when the woman serving him looks good enough to eat.

I pushed through the crowd to see which bartender was outperforming the rest, and when I saw her, her presence gripped me by the throat and pulled me closer. My eyes slid down her body of their own accord and for the first time I could remember, I wasn't in control.

She had wild blonde hair streaked with honey highlights. A smattering of freckles ran across her nose and cheeks, just visible in the dim light behind the bar. Her bee-stung lips curved into a smile as a patron leaned over and left his number scratched across a cocktail napkin. She didn't touch it. She was too busy straining a drink into a cocktail glass. The two male bartenders moved around her, cashing out customers and keeping track of the orders. Apparently, the customers wanted their drinks made by her and *only her*.

I watched her spin around and reach for a top-shelf liquor. The sharp cut of the Provisions uniform exposed most of her tan back. The skirt hugged her hips and flared just below her ass. On her, it looked like glorified lingerie.

I should have backed away and found Zoe. I knew what was pulling customers toward the bar and I could move onto the next item on my agenda. Lord knows I had a list a mile long, and yet, I found myself stepping closer to the bar. I slid onto a free stool directly in front of where she was making drinks and waited for her undivided attention.

Because she was a complete knockout?

No.

Because she was utterly fucking up my bar.

CHAPTER FOUR

LILY

IN THE LAST two hours the bar had turned into a circus. I'd lost track of how many drinks I'd made. My feet hurt, my hands ached, and I'd gone through enough lemons and limes to rival a key lime pie factory. The only silver lining was the tip jar steadily filling up smack dab in front of me. Whenever exhaustion started to creep in, I'd let my gaze linger there for a second. I'd have to split it all with Brian and Allen, but still, my cut would be massive.

I handed two drinks off, shook the excess club soda from my hand, and then watched as a suited man slipped into a newly vacant bar stool. He wasn't the first available guy to come to the bar, but he was the first one who made me do a double take. I had a very specific type, and pretty boys were out—I didn't want a guy with better hair than me. (*Jared Leto, I'm lookin' at you.*)

Suit Guy's features weren't pretty, they were striking.

21

Rough around the edges with a permanent scowl and punch-you-in-the-gut brown eyes. His dirty blond hair was unruly and probable evidence of a bad habit of running his hands through it when he was stressed.

I opened my mouth to ask him his drink order, but another customer spoke up first.

"What was that drink you made me earlier?" the young girl beside him asked, swaying her empty cocktail glass back and forth in front of her like a fast-paced metronome. I'd made her a drink hours ago; I had a good memory, but not *that* good.

"Describe it," I said, leaning forward so I could hear her over the sound of the crowd. The effort brought me closer to Suit Man and it annoyed me that I noticed his cologne. *Or maybe I'm annoyed that I liked it.*

"You recommended it," the girl slurred. "It was like a pineapple made love to a boozy banana."

I ran through the drinks I'd made earlier in the night that had pineapple in them. There'd only been a few, and the cocktail glass she was waving around helped me narrow it down.

"It's called a Juliet," I told the customer, already reaching for a new cocktail glass. "It has gold tequila, banana-flavored liqueur, pineapple juice, and grenadine."

Her eyes widened. "Yes! More please!"

I smiled and turned to the bar shelves to reach for the gold tequila. Suit Man spoke up behind me and my back stiffened.

"I don't see that drink on the menu…"

His voice was sexy, but his tone sounded seriously annoyed.

I glanced over my shoulder at him. "No. It's just something I like to make."

His dark brow arched as he assessed my answer. "The city's top mixologist spent weeks crafting this drink list."

Top mixologist? I had flipped through the leather-bound list earlier, completely uninspired by the generic drinks. I'd assumed it was thrown together by some busboy that had Googled "how to make hipster cocktails".

I set the gold tequila down on my station and shrugged. "I like to play by own rules."

Brian came up behind me, nearly shoving me out of the way to reach Suit Man.

"Sir, I didn't see you there. Can I get you anything? The usual?"

I smirked. The guy must be one hell of a tipper to elicit that sort of ass-kissing from Brian.

"No. I'd actually like *her* to make me a drink," he said with a dark tone.

I was looking down, measuring out a shot of tequila, or he would have seen my eyes narrow. *What is his angle?*

"Lily," Brian whispered under his breath, trying to get my attention.

I glanced over at him from beneath my lashes. His eyes widened as he inclined his head toward the man. The message was clear: make his drink. *Now.*

Unfortunately, I'd never been very good at taking orders.

I plastered on a fake smile and met Suit Man's annoyed stare.

"I'll be happy to take your order, right after I finish up with these fine folks who were here before you." My tone was clipped and cool, but no one could accuse me of being outright rude. It was the voice adopted by anyone who'd ever had to work a shift in a service job.

Suit Man sat and watched me mix three more drinks. I

23

was still faster than Brian, but compared to earlier, I was taking my sweet time. His dark eyes stayed pinned on me as anger palpably boiled off of him. I selected my ingredients with care and measured them out like I was creating a work of art.

I caught fragments of his shattering composure as I twisted and turned behind the bar: his clenched, clean-shaven jaw; the gap in the top of his shirt where his tensed, tan chest peeked through; his knuckles, motionless but growing whiter as he gripped the edge of the bar.

By this time, the crowd around the courtyard had diminished, which left Brian with no other orders to busy himself with.

"Sir, are you sure I can't get you anything?" Brian asked, his voice a tad more shrill than it'd been only minutes before. "Seriously, Lily—"

Suit Man shook his head, leaned forward, and propped his elbows on the bar.

"Brian, go clean up the other end of the bar," he ordered.

I met his stare and took off the friendly mask I usually wore for customers. Our eyes locked with unspoken fury. I'd been on my feet all night, I was exhausted, and now I had to deal with a customer from hell. He had no clue who he was dealing with.

"Make me a Collins," he said through seductive lips. They were the sort of lips made for giving orders and delivering on promises.

He offered no please. No thank you.

I held his stare as I reached for a highball glass. I took pride in every drink I made, but I knew his drink would be irre-fuckin-proachable. I expertly poured two ounces of dry gin by sight, and then added a touch more. One teaspoon of superfine sugar and half an ounce of lemon juice went into the glass next. I stirred it all together and spritzed it with a touch of club soda. He took the glass out of my hand before I could slide it across the bar. I watched him bring it to his lips, holding back every snarky remark that came to mind.

"Too heavy on the sugar," he declared, dropping the glass back onto the bar. "Make it again."

He'd hardly taken a sip.

I had to bite down on my tongue until I nearly drew blood. *The customer is always right. Even if the customer is full of shit, he's always right.*

"Are you for real?" a nearby customer asked in my defense before turning to me. "Don't worry girl, your bartending skills are on point. Don't listen to him."

Mr. Suit didn't acknowledge her and I knew I had no choice. I had to make it again.

I measured out the ingredients into a new glass as my hand shook with anger. I held out the drink again, ignoring the touch of his fingers as he pulled it from my grasp. His brows furrowed into a line as he took a belt of the new drink. I watched him and waited for him to concede and thank me for the second drink.

He shook his head. "Not enough lemon."

I could count on one hand the number of times I'd had a customer ask me to remake a drink. He didn't know what he was talking about. I reached across the bar and took the glass out of his hand. His jaw dropped.

"Lily! Jesus," Brian said, trying to pull the drink out of my hand. I held on to the glass and watched the man's nostrils flare as I took a sip of my own creation. It was good. Chilled and flavorful.

"You are impossible," I hissed. "Sorry, but we don't need your money this badly."

He smirked and shook his head, reaching into his back pocket. He unfolded his leather wallet and pulled out two one-hundred-dollar-bills. "Wrong. We always want the customer's money." He tossed the bills across the bar and scooted his bar stool back. "You're fired. Consider that your severance."

My heart leapt to my throat.

Wait.

What?

"Dude, you're oblivious," Brian moaned. "Do you know who that was?"

I could barely hear Brian through the ether; I was too focused on the man slipping back through the crowd.

He was just another customer…right?

"That was Dean Harper." He laughed, answering his own question. "It was nice knowin' you."

CHAPTER FIVE

DEAN

Zoe: You didn't fire the new girl did you? Tell me you aren't that stupid.

I ignored Zoe's text and laced up my beaten-up running shoes. My phone buzzed again and I reluctantly read the text.

Zoe: The bar brought in four times the amount it usually does last night. JUST FYI.

Zoe had been with my team for the last five years. We worked well together because she was a good manager and one hundred percent uninterested in me—*or any other man for that matter*. I brought her in as a temporary manager at the start of every restaurant. She helped me hire and train the new staff for the first few weeks, and she was damn

27

good at her job. Her knack for annoying banter was *not* why I kept her around.

Zoe: Why'd you do it?

I would have ignored her question, but something told me she wouldn't stop until I appeased her.

Dean: She's not Provisions material.

My phone buzzed instantly.

Zoe: Yeah, you're right. Making money is overrated.

I plugged my headphones in and pulled up my workout playlist. Zoe could text her fingers raw, but I had to start my run. My calves were tight from my last workout, but the tension would ease up by the time I reached the park. I locked up my apartment and slipped my spare key into the laces of my left shoe. Then, I took off.

I had to do some form of exercise every day, and I wasn't particularly committed to one specific thing. Running, biking, rowing, anything that got my limbs moving made it easier to tame the fire burning inside me. I'd pound the pavement and feel the pieces of my life fall into place.

I'd thought I'd be happy after I made my first million, my tenth, my twentieth. I'd thought by the time I had a solid grip on New York's restaurant scene, I'd be satisfied. I was wrong. The fire never died and I always wanted more.

Any freshman in college with a handful of psychology credits could connect the dots that I was using work to fill an emotional void in my life, but objectively speaking, they had to be wrong. I didn't have voids. I'd had more than my fair share of women and I'd even truly loved one or two of them along the way. I yearned for nothing, lacked for nothing, and yet still, I pushed myself harder.

Why?

Because some people just like a challenge.

I was rounding a trail in Central Park when my phone buzzed with an incoming call. I checked it, prepared to ignore Zoe again, but Julian's name popped up instead.

"Julian, what's up?" I asked, using the opportunity to catch my breath. I was only halfway done with my run, but I stretched my hamstring with my free hand, careful not to overextend the muscle.

"Hey man, are you back in town?" he asked.

"Landed last night."

"Let me guess, you went straight to work, barely slept, and now you're what—working out?"

I smirked. Julian and I had been friends since college. He knew my habits better than anyone. "Touché, jackass. What do you want?"

He laughed and then I heard a female voice in the background. Likely, he was with his girlfriend, Josephine.

"I'm over at Central Park taking pictures for Jo's blog. You should come by. I think we're going to head to breakfast after we get all the shots she needs."

I couldn't do breakfast, but I was already in Central Park. It wouldn't hurt to stop by for a few minutes. I'd finish the other half of my run afterward.

"Where are you?"

"Lower east side, right by 72nd."

I glanced up at the street sign. I was at 66th and Broadway, so if I cut straight over, I'd be there in no time.

"All right, see you in a sec."

Central Park was packed with families and tourists trying to make the most of their Saturday morning. In a few hours, the park would almost be too hot to inhabit, but with the sun hidden behind townhouses to the east, the temperature was still cool. I slowed to a walk when I neared 72nd Street and scanned the park for Julian and Josephine. I rounded Rumsey Playfield, and then kept walking along the trail. I was just about to hit 5th Avenue when I heard laughter.

"Lily. Shut up! I can't take serious pictures if you're making jokes the whole time."

"What am I supposed to do?! Your face looks weird! I said to look like a tiger, not a constipated house cat."

I veered toward the voices and scanned the trail until I spotted them off to the side, nearly hidden in the trees. Josephine posed up on a rock with the forest as her backdrop. She was dressed to the nines for her fashion blog and an unfamiliar blonde was snapping photos of her a few feet away. Julian stood off to the side, probably trying to stay out of the line of fire.

"Try doing something like this," the blonde said, angling her body into a pose I'd seen celebrity women do a thousand times. The effort revealed an inch of tantalizing skin between her jean shorts and her white shirt. The simple outfit and her matching pair of Converse reminded me of the girls back home in Iowa.

I took a step closer, paused my music, and wrapped my headphones around my neck. My movement caught Josephine's attention; she grinned and hopped off the rock. "The titan of industry made it!"

"Hey Jo," I said before throwing Julian a nod.

Her photographer was the last one to turn to greet me.

She was tinkering with the camera, staring down at it so that her hair covered nearly half her face. I focused on the half I could see, that single high cheekbone and the pink lips that curved into a smile.

I took another step closer and she glanced up, lazily flicking her gaze up my workout shorts and tank. I recognized her a moment before she made the connection; when my identity finally sank in for her, a flame flared behind her bright eyes.

"What the fuck are you doing here?" she asked.

CHAPTER SIX

LILY

DEAN HARPER HAD some fucking nerve. (And a seriously toned physique, if you were someone who paid attention to that kind of thing. I, of course, could not have cared less.) After he'd axed me the previous evening I'd known that we were bound to have a run-in sometime. I just hadn't anticipated that it would happen the very next morning.

I was still licking my wounds for Christ's sake.

I stepped closer and gripped Josephine's camera with enough fury to turn it to dust. She took notice and gently pried it from my fingers before it became a casualty of the turf war that was about to ensue.

To his credit, Dean looked just as pissed as I did. His dark eyes scanned me up and down, seemingly disgusted to see me standing there. "*You're* Lily?"

"Lily Noelle Black," I sneered. "Don't worry, I'm not

offended—it must be so hard for you to keep track of all the people you're an asshole to."

Julian stepped into no-man's land, holding his hands up between us. With his dark hair and chiseled features, he usually seemed intimidating, but in front of Dean, he couldn't compare. They were about the same height, but Dean had more muscle—muscle he probably wanted to use to strangle me at that very moment. "Jesus. What is wrong with you two?" Julian asked. "What happened last night?"

I crossed my arms, cocked my hip, and flashed Dean an *"I got you, bitch"* sort of smirk. "Go ahead, tell them, Dean. For the second time in twelve hours, I yield the floor to you."

Dean tugged his hands through his hair, confirming my suspicion about his habit. Then he pulled his gaze from mine and looked to Julian. For what, solace? Moral support? *Yeah right, bucko.*

"Lily had her first night at Provisions last night and she turned my bar into a Coyote Ugly knockoff."

My eyes bulged out of my face. Literally. They had to have fallen out of my skull in responce to the amount of bullshit he'd just spewed. I glanced at the ground, confirmed my eyeballs were not in fact lying there, and then stepped closer to Dean with my finger pointed right at his chest.

Julian straightened his arms out between us, prepared to keep us apart if it came down to it.

"I did *not* mess up your bar. I made you so much money it's ridiculous!"

Dean's eyes flared with anger. "You insulted my menu in front of the customers! You disrespected me and my staff—"

"Oh c'mon! That drink menu sucks and you know it!

Bahama Mamas? How innovative."

"Okay! Whoa." Josephine stepped in, grabbed me by the upper arms, and cut off my view of Dean's death stare. I focused on her and for the first time since Dean had arrived, I was able to take a calming breath.

"Lily. You need to cool it," she said.

"And Dean," Julian cut in. "What the hell has gotten into you?"

We both grunted in annoyance, so in sync that I would have laughed had I not despised him so much. Jo turned to Julian and they exchanged a worried glance.

"Why don't we go to our separate corners for a bit," Julian suggested.

Jo nodded. "I was thinking the exact same thing."

I hated being patronized. Dean and I didn't need mediators. He and I could work out our problems on our own, but Julian had already turned and directed Dean back to the trail. I watched his back, waiting for him to turn around and throw me one last death stare, but he never turned back and Josephine pulled me away before I could think to hurl one last obscenity his way.

I kicked up dirt on the path, still reeling from the skirmish. Josephine squeezed my shoulder as we walked toward 5th Avenue.

"Wow. So that was—"

I glanced up at her. "Horrific."

She narrowed her eyes. "Colorful."

"You should have seen the way he treated me last night."

She rolled her lips together and slid her green gaze my way. "Well, I can guess that it wasn't very good."

"He pretended to be a shitty customer and then fired me on the spot. Right in front of the other bartenders."

She stopped dead in her tracks. "Seriously?"

I nodded.

"Do you want to go back? I'll hold him down and let you kick his shins."

I smirked. The idea of attacking Dean with Josephine as an accomplice sounded tempting, but there had to be a better way to get under his skin. I just had to think.

"No, it's fine. Let's just go to the apartment. I need to get back to my job search anyway."

I caught her frown out of the corner of my eye. "I'm so sorry Lil, but I can't. Julian and I have breakfast plans with his sister and then she wants to show me some of the designs from her upcoming collection."

I'd been in New York for two days and already I felt like Josephine was too busy for me.

"Will you be back in time for dinner?"

"Vogue bloggers are meeting up for a work happy hour," she recited, eyeing her phone's calendar.

I nodded. Perfect. I had very important plans too. They included: emailing my resume to every restaurant within a one hundred mile radius while streaming a Pretty Little Liars marathon for background noise to fool me into thinking I wasn't alone.

CHAPTER SEVEN

DEAN

"DEAN, YOU HAVE to hire Lily back."

I glared at Julian and he arched his brows for emphasis. "I'm dead serious."

I'd walked with him through the park, explaining my side of the story from the night before. I knew I wasn't on hundred percent in the right, but Lily definitely wasn't an angel. Her attitude? Her personality? She was like a cat backed into a corner: claws out, ready to strike.

"Look, I know she's your friend, and I don't doubt that she's probably a delight to be around most days, but those hotheaded employees never last long. Why do you think I have to work for myself?"

Julian shook his head.

"She just moved from Texas two days ago. She moved in with Jo and needs work. She isn't going to make or break you or your restaurants. This is about helping out a friend."

"Well, you're asking too much of me, man. Josephine? She's like a sweet southern peach. If she needed a job, I'd give her one in a second."

He laughed. "I don't think she'd ditch Vogue to go roll silverware for you."

I clapped my hands. "Well there you have it. The job fair is closed."

"You're being a dick."

I whirled around to face him. "Did you not just listen to me? I-do-not-like-Lily. I'm not going to hire her in my restaurant. Not now. Not ever."

He crossed his arms and studied me. What he was looking for? I had no fucking clue.

"Wipe the slate clean and give her one more chance. You two didn't meet in the best circumstances. Let's go to dinner so that you can both bury the hatchet. If it still doesn't work out after that, fine, but at least you can explain to Josephine that you tried not once, but twice to help Lily out."

I hated being told what to do. Always had. I liked to listen to my own instincts, especially when it came to my companies. Unfortunately, I knew that banishing Lily from my professional life wouldn't matter if she had already spilled over into my personal life. I considered Julian and Josephine to be my closest friends. For that reason—and that reason alone—I nodded and agreed to dinner.

"7 PM Monday. You pick a neutral territory and I want her patted down before I arrive."

CHAPTER EIGHT

LILY

NIGHTS I'D BEEN in New York: 3

Nights Josephine had stayed at Julian's apartment: 3

When I'd pictured my move to New York City, it was Josephine and I taking on the world. I'd had dreams of exploring the city with her. Y'know, experiencing our first mugging together, paying ten bucks in Chinatown to get our hair dyed, and then laughing days later as it all fell out. *See?* Fun! Unfortunately, it looked like I would be exploring the city solo. Sadly, I had the feeling that going bald by myself wouldn't be nearly as amusing.

Josephine had been my best friend since we had buckteeth and Polly Pockets shoved up our noses. I'd made the move to New York City partly for her, but she had a new boyfriend who looked like the offspring of two beautiful soap opera stars, so I was no longer her top priority.

I sighed and shoved my hand back into the cereal box, only to find it empty. *Blast*. I could have wallowed in self-pity for another solid thirty minutes at least, but not without a constant stream of Cinnamon Toast Crunch. I had no choice; I had to leave the apartment.

I crawled toward my suitcase and reached for the first thing my fingers brushed. It was a soft blue t-shirt with a white outline of Texas stretched across the front. In the center, in a bold font, it read "Made".

I cried as I gripped it in my hand. The tears shocked me. They were ugly and loud enough that the neighbors could definitely hear, but I couldn't stop. I was in way over my head. I'd had one job prospect in New York City. Provisions was supposed to provide me with a steady income until I landed something more permanent. Instead, Dean Harper had stomped around like an angry wolf, huffing and puffing and blowing my dreams down before I could even begin to build them. *Wait...that makes me one of the stupid pigs with shitty building materials.* I cried harder.

My phone buzzed on the floor beside me and Josephine's face flashed across the screen. She was asleep in the photo. Her dark hair was sticking up in every direction and I'd drawn male genitalia across her cheeks. It was a photo from our senior year of high school and it still made me laugh.

"What are you doing?" she asked.

I stared down at the Made in Texas shirt. "Nothing."

That sounded lame.

"Working out," I corrected.

"Oh wow, good for you. Cardio? The city has some fun trails."

I rolled my eyes and fell back onto the floor. She was only making me feel worse.

"What are your plans for the day?" I asked.

"I have to do an interview for my Vogue column and then finish up taking those outfit photos from yesterday to post on my blog. Want to hang out later?"

Finally! Light at the end of the tunnel!

"Sounds good."

"K. I'll call you."

She hung up and I stared up at the ceiling, realizing for the first time that I had essentially moved to New York without a solid plan. I'd left everything behind in Texas: my steady but terrible job at Acapulco Tex-Mex Grill, my pile of unfinished Pinterest DIY projects, and a beat-up red car I'd lovingly nicknamed Hoopty.

For what?

To make it in the restaurant industry.

And what was I doing? Throwing the world's biggest pity party. I couldn't give up on my dreams on day three, even if Dean Harper was an asshole and even if Josephine was too busy to actually hang out with me. I'd find a cooler boss than Dean and awesome friends other than Josephine.

I gripped on to that tiny sliver of hope and sat up. I couldn't sit around and wait for my dreams to happen. I had to take life by the horns. I brushed my hair and my teeth, and then threw on a business-casual outfit. Practical, slim-fitting navy slacks, flats, and one of Josephine's white blouses. She at least owed me *that* much.

A little under-eye concealer hid my temporary mental breakdown, and a dab of mascara brought me back to the land of the living.

I felt like I was in a music video as I walked toward the subway station. "You Only Live Once" by The Strokes blasted through my headphones, giving me a little pep in my step.

I was heading down into the subway system for the first time when Josephine texted me. I wasn't sure if I'd lose cell reception down in the depths of Middle Earth—or wherever the subway stairs led—so I slid to the side and pressed up against the subway tiles as I read what she'd sent.

Josephine: Just got word that Julian wants to do dinner tonight. Meet us at Gramercy Tavern around 7? His treat!

Lily: Sounds good.

I smiled. I could brag to them about everything I'd managed to get done that day. *Oh me? I'm just employed at the swankiest restaurant in town and I got invited to Baby Blue Ivy's birthday party. So yeah, killin' it.*

I headed for the bottom of the stairs and paused as I took in the zoo around me. Confident, fast-paced New Yorkers were zooming effortlessly around the subway station. I watched them push their way through metal turnstiles and wondered where they'd acquired their little swipey card things. I turned in a circle, looking for an information booth, but it was hard to see beyond the hordes of people in black, gray, and shades of brown. You would have thought the state had outlawed color. I mean, *really people.*

I tried to catch someone's eye so I could ask for help, but not a single person glanced my way. I was officially on my own. I moved out of everyone's way and was about to search "how to use the NYC subway system" on my phone when I noticed a text Josephine had sent a few minutes earlier.

Josephine: Oh and no big deal, but Dean will be joining us. Okay, bye. TTYL.

"Shit."

"Lady, you okay?"

I glanced away from my phone to find a homeless man sitting on the floor beside me. His white scraggly beard was nearly a foot long and his hair was made up of tight dreadlocks sticking out in every direction. His light grey eyes met mine and I frowned.

"Y'know, not really," I admitted.

He shrugged. "Mama told me there'd be days like that."

I nodded. Wise words for a man wearing a shirt that read "The Blue Bunny Strip Club XXX."

"I'm Lily," I offered, sticking out my hand.

He focused his gaze on my palm, seemingly confused about what to do with it. I wrapped my fingers back into a fist and let my hand fall.

"Nelson," he said with a nod.

"Ever taken the subway?" I asked before glancing back out at the crowd of people.

He spoke with such a thick accent that the words seemed to blend together. "What kind of question is that? You think I hang out down here for the scenery?"

All right then. "I'll buy you a burger if you help me figure it out."

"With cheese?"

I smiled. "Of course."

And that's how Nelson the vagabond became my first friend in New York City. *Hello, full social calendar.*

The Allure of Dean Harper

CHAPTER NINE

LILY

AFTER A FULL day of job-hunting, I turned the corner onto 20th Street and immediately picked up the tantalizing scents filling the air around Gramercy Tavern. A hint of roasted chicken was enough to send my stomach growling for the one-thousandth time that evening. Somewhere between breakfast and dinner, I was supposed to stop and feed myself, but I hadn't had the time. In a moment of weakness, I'd stopped for a hot pretzel from a street vendor, but in another moment of even greater weakness, I'd tripped and dropped the pretzel into a puddle. FML.

I pulled open the heavy wood door and nearly fainted on the spot as the smell of garlic mashed potatoes hit me in full force. *Be still my heart.* There were a dozen people waiting to be seated, all pressed together in the foyer. I pushed through them to find the hostess stand and smiled at the petite blonde ready to jot my name down on her clipboard.

"Hi, how many in your party?"

"Oh, I think there should be a reservation under Mr. Lefr—"

"Lily."

My back stiffened at the sound of my name uttered by a familiar deep voice. *Please be Julian. Please be Julian.* I turned on my heel and came face to face with Dean Harper leaning against the wall of the foyer with his hands stuffed into the pockets of his black slacks. His brows were furrowed, his bow lips were set in a thin line and his brown eyes were emitting disdain on levels that should have been reserved for truly heinous criminals. *Or y'know that annoying person who tries to cut in front of you in the frozen yogurt line. I'm getting toppings, whore. This isn't a free-for-all.*

I took a step toward him and then gawked as the redhead beside him leaned in to kiss his cheek. She was nearly his height, which made her a few inches taller than me, but it was her hair that held my attention. The strands were made of pure fire, the same shade she'd used to coat her lips. Her dress was tight and black, wrapped around her body in a way that made me tug at the simple white blouse I'd put on that morning. I'd run around the city in it for the last twelve hours, so chances were I was sporting approximately two to four mystery stains and enough wrinkles to make it seem as if I'd just pulled it out of the hamper.

"We're waiting on Julian and Jo," Dean said, foregoing any sort of greeting. I glanced back to him and caught the tail end of his perusal of my outfit. I arched a brow as our eyes locked.

"You brought a friend," I said with a polite smile aimed

at the woman to his left.

"A date," he corrected.

Of course.

"Ah, well, I didn't realize we were bringing dates."

He tilted his head to the side and narrowed his eyes at me. "I'm sorry, I'll have Jo clear that with you next time. Just so we're all on the same page." He spoke with unaffected indifference.

I opened my mouth to reply when his date stepped forward and cut the tension brewing between us. "I'm Casey," she said, holding out her hand as a peace offering. Her smile was genuine, albeit a little desperate. I'm sure she felt the awkwardness as much as I did.

"Lily," I said, accepting her handshake and cursing the heavens. *How does someone get hands that soft?*

"Nice to meet you, Lily," she beamed.

She was beautiful and polite; what the hell was she doing with Dean?

"How did you two meet?" I asked, focusing my attention on Casey.

She smiled and reached for his hand so she could twine their fingers together. "It's actually a funny story. I was at a coffee shop, y'know that cool place up on 43rd?" She glanced at Dean. "What's it called?" Before he could reply, she continued the 'funny' story with a wave of her hand. "Anyway, I was ordering a bagel, but I wanted a blueberry one and they were all out of blueberry so then…"

My attention span had been shot somewhere between her first and second sentence, but I pretended to follow along. I didn't need to know her life story. I just wanted to know if he'd somehow drugged her to get her to go out with him.

"And so then anyway, Dean comes up and asks, 'Is this

your coffee'?"

Nope. Still boring. Tune out.

"So yeah!" she said, with a dimpled smile and a shrug, wrapping up her story a few minutes later. "That's about it. I guess this is our second official date."

I smiled, hatching a plan to hit Dean in the wallet. "Well what a special night for you guys. We'd better celebrate. Dean, why don't you order a nice bottle of champagne while we wait?"

"I loooove champagne!" crooned Casey as I grabbed a wine list from the hostess stand.

"I think we should wait for Jul—"

"Nonsense! Casey, would you say you're a light-bodied brut girl?" I asked.

"My favorites are the really bubbly champagnes. I like the way it tickles my nose!" she chirped adorably.

"Bubbly brut, got it." I smiled wide as I found a $600 bottle on the menu. "I think the Selosse would be perfect, don't you agree Dean?"

For a millisecond I thought I spotted a smirk cross Dean's lips, a sly acknowledgement that he knew what game I was playing, but when I glanced back, it was gone. Stoic resolve coated his features, drawing a distinct line between where he stood and where I stood. Apart. Separate. We were practically two different species.

The restaurant's door opened and a frazzled Josephine waltzed in followed by Julian at her heels. They looked love-swept with flushed faces and giant smiles.

"Sorry, sorry, sorry!" Josephine said, squeezing her palms together in a silent prayer that I'd forgive her for being late. "We got held up at the apartment."

I smirked. "Lose the key to the handcuffs again?"

Casey squealed and leaned forward to bat my arm.

"You're *so* bad!"

"Excuse me." The hostess stepped up to our group. "Is everyone in your party present now?"

Dean pushed off the wall. "Yup. Let's get this show on the road." He brushed past me, leaving his date behind in favor of leading the group to our table. I watched him walk, wholeheartedly perplexed by him. The hostess tried to make small talk, but his answers were clipped and disinterested.

"I swear he's not always like this," Josephine whispered as we walked side by side through the restaurant.

I slid my gaze to hers. "You mean he doesn't always exude assholery like it's his job?"

She frowned. "I knew he was a control freak, but I've only been around him when he's in party mode."

I shrugged, sliding my gaze back in his direction. He'd made it to the table a few steps in front of us and was already pulling out a chair.

"Casey," he said abruptly, directing her to take the seat beside him. How politely *controlling* of him.

She sat down like a dutiful date and I nabbed the seat beside her so that I wouldn't split up the two lovebirds. Julian held out Josephine's chair and then leaned down to kiss her hair. She smiled up at him adoringly and my stomach twisted at the site. Envy wasn't a familiar feeling for me and I wasn't sure how to compartmentalize the sensation. Did I want a boyfriend? I hadn't thought of it. I was too busy trying to focus on my career. Would I love a one-night stand? Some kickass sex? Absolutely. Unfortunately, the only bachelor I'd met in New York City was Nelson and something told me I should hold out for a man who'd at least showered in the last month. *Y'know, draw the line somewhere…*

Our waiter appeared in a penguin suit complete with a perfectly placed bow tie. He leaned down to place our menus in front of us and then popped our napkins open with a flourish, draping them over the laps of every female diner. That familiar rush ran through me as I picked up the tavern's menu. I lived for good food. The way some people got runner's highs, I got food highs. Reading over a new menu felt like diving into a new book. At a good restaurant like Gramercy Tavern, the menu told a story—one most people tended to overlook, but not me.

"Good evening, everyone. Our specials for today include a pork bolognese with summer squash and basil. We also have smoked trout with cipollini purée and pickled onions."

"Oh, I've heard good things about the pork bolognese," I said with a smile.

The waiter glanced over at me with an appreciative nod. "It's one of my favorites. I'll give you all a few moments to gather your drink orders and then I'll be back."

Once he was gone, we all returned to perusing the menu.

"What's this?" Josephine asked, leaning toward me and pointing to the first item on the menu.

"It's like a caprese salad, but with sweet peppers added. You'd like it."

She nodded and pointed to the next thing. "And this?"

I laughed and began to explain the dishes to the table, ignoring Dean's glares.

"A restaurant like this is known for their specialty items. I'd skip over the summer greens. It's a glorified salad and you can get that anywhere. For the first course I'd go with the beef tartare or the lobster salad."

"Oh my god that sounds so good." Julian groaned and

rubbed his hand over his stomach.

Josephine dropped her menu and stared my way. "Lily, you order for me. I trust your judgment."

Julian smiled. "Ditto."

Casey glanced over. "Uh, I think I'll trust you too. This menu could be in French and I wouldn't know the difference."

I beamed. Ordering for someone else was like giving them a little present. I'd already looked up the menu when I was waiting for the subway earlier, so I knew what dishes would be the best.

Dean gripped his menu tighter, running his eyes down the list of items. "I'd prefer to order my own food."

Josephine and I exchanged a knowing glance and I held back a laugh. What a shame, though, really. It would have been fun to prove to him that I knew what I was doing.

"Could I start anyone off with a cocktail?" the waiter asked, appearing to the right of Casey with his notepad and pen in hand.

"I'd like a rickshaw," I said with a smile, not bothering with the cocktail menu.

"Oh! What's in that?" Josephine asked.

"Tito's vodka, lime, and fresh basil. It's a good cocktail for the start of a meal. Not too filling."

Julian smiled. "Let's get a round of those for the table then."

Dean spoke up, directing his dark stare at the waiter. "I'll stick with an old fashioned."

Josephine rolled her eyes. "Dean, you're being a stick in the mud."

Casey laughed. "Yeah, I agree. C'mon, babe. It'll be fun if we all get the same drink."

He shook his head and dropped his menu to the table,

clearly struggling to keep his temper at bay. Was it that hard to be at dinner with us? Were we such terrible people to be around? Or was it just me?

I tilted my head and studied him. "No worries, Dean. You order want you want."

"I need your permission even less than I need you to order for me."

Silence hung around the table as we stared each other down. The waiter cleared his throat and then spoke up. "*Okay then*, I'll get the table four rickshaws and one old fashioned."

I held up my finger. "Actually, let's make that *five* rickshaws and an old fashioned. Just in case."

Dean's jaw ticked back and forth as the waiter walked away to fill our drink orders. "There's a fine line between persistence and annoyance."

My cheeks flamed at his critique, but a fire grew in my veins. If he wanted to take this dinner from pleasant to painful, why should I bother doing anything otherwise?

"Is that the same line that falls between being a control freak and just being an asshole?"

"Okay!" Josephine interrupted with a shrill voice. "Let's talk about something else now. Who's watching Game of Thrones? How awesome are Daenerys and her dragons?"

If I had pet dragons, Dean would have already been burned to a crisp long ago.

"I'm going to use the little girls room," Casey said.

I pushed my chair back and stood to join her.

"Mind if I tag along?"

Her smile faltered, but she nodded. I trailed after her, trying to ignore Dean's heavy stare on my back. I'd thought my hatred for the man had reached an all-time high when he'd fired me, but somehow he'd found a way to ensure his spot as number one on my worst enemies list.

I was washing my hands in the sink when I met Casey's eyes in the mirror. Honestly, I couldn't figure out what she was doing with Dean. She was pretty and nice; Dean would suck the life right out of her.

She offered me a tentative smile and before I knew it, evil, albeit funny lies were starting to spill out of my mouth. Dean had played his cards in front of the entire table and now I was going to play mine.

"That's so great that you're willing to date Dean even with the, uh, y'know..." I motioned in a circle below my waist. "...*situation* down there."

She tilted her head with narrowed eyes. "What?"

I shot her a pitying smile. "Yeah. It's pretty bad. He almost lost it all together after the electric shaver incident last year."

She swallowed and then dropped her lipstick back into her purse. Even with her head down I could see her eyes widen in shock.

"Are you serious?"

"Oh no." I clapped my hand over my mouth as if I'd just spoken out of turn. "I'm sure he was going to tell you soon," I said, squeezing her shoulder. "I think he just wanted you to get to know him first."

She groaned and threw her head back. "How long did he think he could go without telling me? Guys like him think they can get away with shit like this just because they're rich."

I nodded as if I completely understood. "I know. Personally, it wouldn't bother me. Except, well, Julian let it slip that Dean refuses to give..." I lowered my voice. "...oral. Even now."

One of Casey's eyelids twitched slightly. "I am so over men in this city."

"Try to cut him some slack. I think he's just guarded after the Russian mail-order bride fell through last year." I sighed. "Anastasya."

Too far? Maybe.

She heaved out a breath and shook her head. "Whatever. I don't need this. I'm a Knicks cheerleader. Do you know how many guys I could get?"

I nodded with an understanding smile. "Hundreds, I bet."

"Thanks for telling me though. Girl code, right?"

I grinned. "Exactly."

We finished primping. She let me borrow some of her red lipstick and I swiped it across my pout, feeling as if I'd just played a winning hand. My hair looked good and there was a healthy glow on my cheeks from walking around the city all day.

Was I being devious by sabotaging Dean's date?

Without a doubt.

Did I feel guilty as I left the bathroom with Casey on my heels?

I'd never felt so good. Being a diabolical villain was definitely a good look for me.

CHAPTER TEN

DEAN

DINNER WAS GOING terribly. Honestly, George R.R. Martin's red wedding had fewer awkward moments than that evening. When Casey and Lily returned from the bathroom, Casey pulled her phone out of her purse and focused intently on the screen like a sixteen-year-old out at dinner with her parents. I tried to get her attention, but she waved me off as her fingers flew over her iPhone. When I glanced up around the table, Lily was trying to hide a smirk and doing a fairly shitty job of it.

Josephine was busy talking about her job, but I knew Lily wasn't listening. She stared down at her fingers, twisting them up in her napkin. I knew she'd said something to Casey in the bathroom, I just didn't know what.

She glanced up and saw me watching her. I narrowed

my eyes and she mirrored my expression. It was a silent duel with no witnesses and no judges, but I'd be damned if I let her win.

"All right, here are those drinks," the waiter announced, leaning over Lily to place her drink to the side of her plate. He followed the pattern around the table, handing me my old fashioned, and then faltering when he got to the extra rickshaw. Lily met my eyes and quirked a brow. I leaned back in my chair and took a deep swallow of my old fashioned. It was perfect, familiar, and most importantly, what *I'd* ordered.

Lily flashed the waiter a kind smile. "You can set it in the middle. I'm sure someone will drink it."

I'd only been around Lily three times, but I could already pinpoint what it was about her that irked me: she was opinionated and too stubborn for her own good.

"Y'know, I think your drink choice says a lot about you," Lily said from the opposite side of the table. Casey slipped her phone into her purse and glanced up, clearly aware that there was about to be a scene. I knew better than Lily. We wouldn't get along, we wouldn't be friends. The best thing to do at a dinner like this would be to ignore each other, but Lily kept pushing my buttons.

"How so?" Casey asked when I didn't take the bait.

I rolled my eyes.

"Perhaps Dean's a little old fashioned himself? Set in the old way of doing things?"

"I disagree. I'd say I'm quick to make changes when things…or people…just aren't working out. The other night, for example."

She leaned forward over the table. "How much money did my section bring in, Dean? Two? Three times the amount each bar usually cashes out?"

I'd checked the numbers the morning after I'd fired her; Zoe hadn't exaggerated. Lily's section had brought in four times the amount the other bars had and I had no doubt she could have cashed out with even more had I not fired her in the middle of her shift.

"Tell me, Lily. How many restaurants have you opened?" I asked with a sharp tone.

Her eyes shifted down to the white tablecloth and then back up to me—a simple tell that her confidence wasn't impenetrable.

"That's—"

"How many bars? Lounges?" I narrowed my eyes. "Have you ever managed more than a handful of stoned high schoolers at a Dairy Queen?"

Her cheeks flamed red beneath her tan and my conscience warned me to back down. Most of the time Lily acted as if she could spar with the best of them, but I knew her armor had weak points. She was a disobedient puppy, all bark and no bite.

I took a deep breath. "The point is, until you've attempted to run a restaurant in New York City, you won't fully understand all the reasons why I had to let you go."

Her eyes seared a line of fire across the table and I watched her chest rise and fall in quick successions. I'd pushed too far.

"Y'know, suddenly I've lost my appetite." She scraped her chair back from the table and stood. Her napkin fell to the ground as she pulled her purse from the back of the chair and crossed it over her body.

"Actually, I think I'll come with you," Casey said, rising from her seat beside me.

What the fuck is going on?

"Uh, I…" Josephine stood and froze, unsure if she

should leave with her friend or stick by Julian.

Lily didn't bother waiting to find out. She turned and spun toward the front of the restaurant with Josephine and Casey on her heels. I felt like a royal ass watching them leave.

Lily brought out my worst qualities. I couldn't remember ever having driven someone to leave a dinner, but she was gone and I was left at the table with that damn rickshaw staring back at me. Condensation gathered on the side of the glass, taunting me until I picked it up and downed it in one long sip.

Damn.

It was good. Better than my old fashioned.

"That was a disaster," Julian said quietly, rubbing his fingers across his chin.

I shrugged. "It wasn't that bad."

He grunted. "You weren't sitting in my seat. Watching you and Lily fight like that isn't fun. I've never seen you like that."

I flinched. "Are you kidding me? Don't put this shit on me."

He shook his head and leaned forward to rest his elbows on the table. I reached for Casey's unfinished rickshaw, downing it too. I had three empty glasses in front of me, but I still wasn't calm. Julian and I sat in silence for a few minutes, and when I finally spoke up, I steered the conversation into more neutral territory.

"We need to have our first meeting for the new restaurant soon. Y'know, start going over expectations and timelines." A few weeks back, Julian had agreed to be a major investor in my next restaurant. I'd presented him with the numbers from my past projects and walked him through the basic steps of opening up a new restaurant. It'd only taken a few minutes to convince him to buy in.

He frowned. "You're putting me in a tough position here, man. Look, I'm not in the restaurant industry. Opening up a new restaurant with you was supposed to be a fun side project. I wanted to work with you as a friend but I'm already catching shit from Jo about this Lily situation. It's just not worth it to me if it's going to cause problems between Jo and Lily."

"Are you serious?" I asked, gripping the edge of the table.

He'd walk away and pull his funding because Lily and I didn't get along? That'd delay the project. I was already putting up 50% of the capital. I'd have to scramble to find more investors if Julian walked.

Before I could plead my case, our waiter stepped up to the table and started clearing away the empty glasses. "Could I get you gentlemen anything else?"

"Just the check," I replied, already reaching for my wallet in my back pocket.

His smile fell. "Uh, actually sir, your guest, the blonde woman? She covered the check on her way out."

I frowned. "Excuse me?"

He swallowed and nodded. "She, er, she actually told me to tell you that it was paid with her *severance*." He whispered the last word as if it was offensive. "I wasn't going to mention it, but..."

I held up my hand to silence him. The night needed to end. I stood and pushed back from the table, thankful that I'd valeted my car around the corner. I wanted to get behind the wheel and press my foot down on the gas until I could feel control fill my veins once again.

"Julian, you can do whatever you want. I'd love to have you on board for this project, but I'm not going to beg. The numbers are there. You'll make back everything you invest by the end of the year. After that? The sky's the limit."

He stood and shrugged on his leather jacket. "Yeah well, you'd make my decision a lot easier if you could just get along with Lily."

I thought back to the way she'd looked at me earlier. Full lips tugged into a frown. Wide, bright eyes narrowed into slits. A rosy tinge marring her tan cheeks.

"It'll never happen."

CHAPTER ELEVEN

DEAN

I WAS ON hour ten of a fifteen-hour workday when Zoe waltzed into the manager's office at Provisions.

"Of course, please, let yourself in and start disrupting me. I was hoping to stretch this into an all-nighter."

My words dripped with sarcasm, but they didn't deter Zoe. She plopped down on the leather seat opposite mine and kicked her feet up onto the desk. "I don't know what you're talking about." She leaned forward and grabbed the heavy metal paperweight she always liked to toy with. "I just like to watch how the master works."

The air conditioning kicked on and half a dozen papers flew off my desk. I didn't even blink. "Pick those up, put the paperweight back, and get your feet off my desk. They smell."

She grunted as she bent down to retrieve the spreadsheets I'd just reviewed. "I think that stench is actually your attitude. It's been rotten ever since you got back from Nebraska."

"Iowa," I corrected, licking my finger and flipping through the resumes in front of me.

She frowned. "There's a difference? I thought it was all just corn fields."

I smirked. "Good point."

"Y'know Provisions has done really well for its first month. Better than you projected."

She was right. The restaurant was killing it. The money we'd invested in advertising was really paying off. "How's it going out front? Staff responding well to the management and everything?" I asked.

She grunted. "Oh, sure. It's great except for the fact that I just had to tend bar for the last six hours. I'll take 'Jobs I'm Overqualified For' for 500, Alex."

I laughed. "I appreciate you helping out, but you'll be happy to know that I just hired two new bartenders this afternoon. I'll need you to get Brian to go over the basics with them before they're put on the floor tomorrow."

She sighed with relief and sunk farther into her chair. Her hair seemed even shorter than usual, framing the feminine features she tried so hard to hide.

"Y'know, I still haven't forgiven you for what you did the other night."

My eyebrows rose with curiosity. "With Lily?"

"Yes with Lily! She was gold, my friend. You should have talked to me before you had your little hissy fit."

I shook my head. "Not you too, Zoe. I'm seriously sick of being scolded."

She laughed. "Then maybe stop acting like a child."

We sat in silence for a moment. I was too annoyed to speak, and she was trying to fight the smirk spreading across her lips.

"You find her attractive don't you?"

I sighed, deeply and heavily.

"C'mon, admit it," she prodded.

"I actually haven't thought about it."

"Uh huh," she nodded, calling my bluff. "Close your eyes."

"Zoe, get out of my office. I have work to do."

She stood and leaned over the table. "Humor me."

I shook my head. "You're being ridiculous."

Her thin lips curled into a smirk, but she held her ground. I knew from experience that Zoe wasn't going to leave. She'd once made me stand outside of a restaurant for thirty minutes because she'd thought she'd seen Lady Gaga walk in. Spoiler: it wasn't her.

I huffed out a breath and closed my eyes, fully expecting her to laugh. Instead, her voice filled my office, reminding me of the one person I'd tried all day to forget about.

"Picture Lily standing at your office door. She's patiently waiting for you to finish up your paperwork so the two of you can head out to dinner. She dressed up for you, wearing something dark, and short, and tempting. Her hair is down and wild. Blonde in a shade that can't be bought in a bottle. Her brown eyes find you behind your desk and she smirks, knowing you've been waiting all day to see her. You drag your eyes down her body—"

"Zoe," I interrupted, keeping my eyes closed. "Do you think she could be holding food? I'm really hungry and in my fantasy, I'd really love a bacon cheeseburger."

She groaned and I opened my eyes to see her heading toward the door of my office with crossed arms. "No really, Zoe. Keep going, but now can you describe the burger?"

She flipped me the bird and rounded the corner out of my office. "What kind of cheese does it have 'cause I really hate American!"

I laughed as she slammed my office door shut, but I wasn't fooling anyone. Of course I knew Lily was gorgeous. I had every contour of her heart-shaped face memorized. Contained within it were the most kissable set of lips I'd ever seen and bright eyes that saw right through my bullshit. I replayed the scene Zoe had created for me. Lily standing in my office door in a little black dress was a fantasy too sweet to comprehend.

If only she and I could shut up for ten minutes, the sex would be the best of our lives. Angry. Hard. Fast. Not love. Not even close.

War.

CHAPTER TWELVE

DEAN

I GLANCED UP from the resume in my hand to take in the nervous candidate sitting across from me. He'd been in my office for five minutes and already my patience was wearing thin.

"Where did you attend culinary school?"

"What school?" he asked, seemingly confused by the question.

"Cul-in-aaarrry school," I repeated, stressing the phonetics of a word I shouldn't have been explaining.

"Ah, yes. Well no, I didn't go."

"Have you worked in any upscale restaurant before?" I asked.

He shook his head, just as confused as before. I sighed and tossed his resume onto my desk. It topped the list of under-qualified applicants for the day.

"Perfect, you can see yourself out."

His lip quivered, but I couldn't muster an ounce of sympathy. I was looking for a consultant for my next restaurant and I'd just spent the morning interviewing a slew of idiots.

"Alright, bud, let's go," Zoe said, stepping into my office. She'd been hovering by the door for the last few interviews.

"Is the interview over?" he asked, glancing back and forth between us. I couldn't confidently say he even knew what planet he was on at that point.

He stood and she directed him out of my office.

By the time I finished shredding his resume, Zoe was back at my office door, hovering on the threshold until I invited her inside.

"I cannot believe you let that guy through," I said.

She frowned. "To be honest, we've had so few people send in applications, I was just hoping that by some miracle, one of them would be qualified."

"That last guy is almost thirty and has never had a job."

She laughed. "Point taken."

I leaned back in my chair and dragged my hand through my hair. "I need a beer."

"I'd buy you one but I have a hot date later."

My brows rose.

"You know, you could have one too if only you'd admit your attraction for a certain blonde."

"Zoe."

She laughed. "Oh my god, it's just too easy with you. Why can't you admit you find her attractive? I won't tell anyone."

I stood and ushered her out of my office, ignoring her protests. I locked myself inside, but she was persistent.

"You're not fooling me," she said.

"Goodnight Zoe," I shouted through the dark wood.

Her laughter faded down the hallway, leaving me alone with the thoughts she'd just planted in my head. It'd been three days since Zoe had first brought Lily to my attention. Since then, I couldn't stop thinking of her full lips wrapped around me. I couldn't stop daydreaming about her. I wasn't proud of it, *believe me*. Lily would have me boiled alive if she knew I was fantasizing about her.

I reached for my phone on my desk, looking for a distraction, but there was nothing there waiting for me. I'd invited Julian to a sports bar near my house for dinner, but he'd yet to reply. I knew it was because he was walking a thin line. Lily hated me, therefore Josephine hated me, which put Julian between a rock and a hard place.

I tossed my phone back onto my desk and clenched my teeth together. Every single problem in my life was being caused by one woman: Lily Black. She was forcing Julian into an ultimatum and I was on the losing end of the deal.

I leaned back in my chair, interlocked my fingers behind my head, and caught sight of Sun Tzu's "The Art of War" on my office shelf. The book highlighted troop movements and battlefield strategies, but more importantly, it stressed one simple idea: *"Know thyself, know thy enemy."*

I smirked.

As much as I hated to admit it, Lily knew a hell of a lot about food and drinks. She'd impressed me at Gramercy Tavern, and she had twice the education of most applicants sending in their resumes for the consulting position. On top of that, I needed to keep Julian as an investor for the project.

I shredded the rest of the applications and pulled "The Art of War" off my shelf. It was settled. I was going to have to convince Lily to work for me. It was time to get to know the enemy.

CHAPTER THIRTEEN

LILY

"NO! NO! YOU do not get to live here," I yelled, running after the cockroach attempting to take up residence in mine and Jo's apartment. I lunged to drop a cup over it, but it scurried under our shared dresser. "No! Get out of there!"

There was an inch of blackness beneath the dresser and the floor and I would have rather cut my hand off than put it under there. He'd won the battle, but I'd win the war.

"Yeah, and stay there!" I yelled, kicking the dresser with my foot. *That's good. Intimidate him.*

I turned back to the sink full of dishes I'd been cleaning before my little friend had interrupted me. Plates and cups were piled high thanks to the mess Josephine and I had created the night before. Julian had requested a home-cooked meal, but Josephine and I hadn't been able to agree on what to make, so we'd each made our favorite dishes (chicken spaghetti for her, and homestyle mac 'n' cheese for me). We'd hovered over him as he ate, watching him carefully as he spooned the bites into his mouth.

"Uh they're both good?" he said, shifting his gaze back and forth between us.

I slammed my hand down on the counter like a disgruntled detective. "Don't you lie to me, Lefray!"

He laughed. "I swear, they're both equally delicious."

I shook my head. "This isn't over. I'm watching you."

Josephine leaned in and kissed his cheek. "I know you'll tell me the real winner later."

"Oh my god." I covered my eyes and backed away slowly. "You guys are like two slobbering wildebeests in heat."

After two more episodes of The Office (first season, of course), they left. It's not like the three of us could all share the one futon, but it still made me sad to lock the door behind them. I hurried to the window and watched them hail a cab. It pulled up to the curb and Julian opened the door for Jo, sweeping a kiss across her lips before they slid into the back together. They weren't slobbering wildebeests. They were the cutest people in the entire world and they made me almost sick with envy every time I saw them doting over one another. When was the last time I'd had a relationship like that? I think I had shown that much affection to a Snicker's ice cream bar once, but it had been a tragically one-sided affair. I'd never loved a man like she loved Julian.

I scrubbed away remnants of cheese from a plate and then caught movement to my right.

"No! You're not allowed out!" I yelled at the cockroach. "God, at least wait until I leave."

A loud knock sounded at the apartment door and I

jumped, dropping the plate into the sink full of suds. *Did Josephine forget her keys?*

"Lily! Open up!"

Oh shit. The police?

"Lily!"

It wasn't until my name was yelled a second time that I registered the familiar deep voice.

Dean *motherfucking* Harper was at my apartment. I'd have preferred the cops.

I swallowed and wiped my pruney hands on the dishrag beside the sink. Okay. He was at my apartment, which meant he probably wanted to talk to me. Or maybe he just needed to get a clipping of my hair for the voodoo doll he was undoubtedly creating so he could continue torturing me from afar.

I walked to the door as he kept hammering away on the thin particleboard.

"What do you want?" I asked, peering through the tiny peephole. He was leaning against the door with his head down. His dirty blond hair was disheveled and curling at the ends. He'd foregone his normal uniform for a t-shirt and running shorts. He looked sweaty, even through the peephole. *Oh god.* He'd run to my apartment.

"Just let me in. We need to talk."

He already sounded pissed and we hadn't even seen each other yet.

"Sorry, no hablo ingles."

"Lily."

"I don't want any Girl Scout cookies. Go away."

"Oh hello there!" a feminine voice chimed from down the hall. I stood on my tiptoes again and peered through the peephole. Oh dear lord, it was Ms. Whittaker, our landlady. Josephine had warned me about her immediately upon my arrival in New York City. She seemed old and endearing, but then she'd invited Jo to a party. She'd gone, assuming it would be a bunch of old people playing Monopoly. Instead, she'd found herself politely navigating her way through a swinger's party. Ms. Whittaker was one kinky old lady.

"Oh hello," Dean replied with a nod.

"Friend of Josephine's?" she asked, pausing mid-step to take him in from head to toe. I held back a snicker.

"Something like that," he answered.

She smirked and stepped closer. "Well, a friend of Josie's is a friend of mine. Say, I host these parties every weekend up on the—"

"He doesn't want to go to your weird swinger parties, Ms. Whittaker!" I yelled through the door.

She shrugged and offered him one final creepy smile before continuing down the stairs. "Mmm, I'll let him make that decision on his own. I'm up on the top floor, sugar."

Dean nodded and stepped back to clear a path for her.

"Have a good day, Lily. Don't forget I need you and Josephine's rent check by the end of next week."

"Got it," I said.

Once she was out of sight, I stepped away from the peephole, unlocked the door, and swung it open a few inches. I wedged my face between the door and the doorframe and waited for him to explain himself. His gaze slid down what was visible of my body, inspecting the oversized t-shirt I was wearing as a nightgown.

"You have ten seconds," I declared.

"Cute shirt."

"It's my dad's," I explained, tugging at the hem. Had I known he was coming over, I would have gotten dressed, and maybe put on a helmet and shin guards—

anything to protect me in our inevitable battle.

The corner of his mouth curled up and he stepped forward pushing the door open with his palm.

"Hey! Just wait a second!" I yelled as he continued to see himself into my apartment. "I didn't invite you in."

I closed the door and then turned to him with an accusatory stare.

"Lily, the sooner you let me talk, the sooner I'll be out of here."

I flung my arms open. "Oh well please speak, because I can't think of a single reason why you"—I stuck my finger in his chest—"being here"—I pointed the other finger at the ground—"makes any sense at all."

He turned to walk through my apartment—which was a glorified shoebox—running his finger over the countertop before inspecting it. *Are you kidding me?* Who did he think he was? He turned back and stared at the futon, still pulled out flat with my pillow and butterfly blanket thrown haphazardly on top. *Add that to the list of things I would have hidden had I known Dean was coming over.*

"I'd like to hire you as a consultant for my new restaurant." He spoke with utter sincerity.

Even still, I barked out a laugh. "Are you smoking crack?"

He frowned. "I'm serious. I don't have any other options and neither do you."

"The hell I do! Just yesterday I interviewed for four different jobs."

Two of which were at Subway (*different locations*), but he didn't need to know that.

He crossed his arms, standing his ground on our tiny battlefield. God he consumed the space, making it his own. His body wash filled the air, mixed with the sweat from his run. When he left, I'd have to light a thousand candles and invite the shaman that lived down the hall to rid the apartment of his aura.

"Julian is the primary investor for the project, and I don't want our differences to jeopardize that. We might not ever learn to get along, but I can at least offer you a job."

Wow. How very *noble* of him.

"Fuck you. I hope Julian walks and you lose the money."

He narrowed his eyes. "Look, I'm not going to beg."

I crossed my arms. "Then don't."

"The job comes with a thousand dollar signing bonus, benefits, and a starting salary of ninety thousand. If you prove your worth, I'll likely consider you for future projects."

His brown eyes seared into me, daring me to turn down the offer.

"And what about us?" I asked. "How are we going to work together?"

He took a deep breath, his broad chest rising and falling as he considered my question. "Y'know, I've dealt with several asshole contractors and plenty of bitchy wait staff. You, *Lily Black*, are nothing I haven't handled before."

A slow smirk spread across my lips. He thought he had me figured out. He thought he had the upper hand.

How cute.

"Well, seeing as how you're out of options, make that a hundred thousand starting salary. And I want one percent of profits for any projects we collaborate on. And before you say I'm just taking advantage of your predicament, just wait a few weeks. Trust me—I'm worth every penny."

The more I pushed him, the tighter he clenched his jaw.

"Deal. I'll have my lawyer draw up the contract tomorrow. Meanwhile, there's a team meeting in the morning at Provisions. 8 AM sharp," he declared as he moved toward the door with long strides. He was done with me for the day. I kept my focus on the tiny window above my sink, trying hard to control my pounding heart. Just as I thought he'd yank open the door and make his exit out of my apartment, his hand hit my elbow. He gripped the soft skin just below the sleeve of my t-shirt.

I shivered at the sensation of his mouth behind my ear, too close for comfort.

"And just so we're clear." He spoke as a helpless ripple traveled down my spine. "This isn't a truce."

CHAPTER FOURTEEN

LILY

BEING ROOMATES WITH Josephine had certain perks. She was tall enough to reach the cereal boxes on the top shelf of our pantry and she had a never-ending supply of designer clothes. As an in-house blogger for Vogue, she got to raid their closet for her weekly blog posts. Next season's Valentino? Special collection Manolo Blahniks? Nothing was off limits to her, which meant nothing was off limits to me.

"How about this sleeveless wrap dress with a cardigan in case you get chilly?"

I glanced up to see Josephine holding a sky blue dress. The cotton material looked soft enough to sleep in, but the cut and design made it fancy enough for work.

"It's gorgeous, but will it be too long on me?"

"Nah. It's way too short on me. That's why I haven't worn it yet."

I held it up against my body and stepped in front of our floor-length mirror.

"Are you nervous?" Josephine asked, stepping up behind me.

"A little bit," I admitted. "But Julian will be there to help ease the pain of working for Dean."

Jo laughed. "I'm still kind of shocked you agreed."

I arched a brow. "It's not like restaurants were knocking down my door or anything. I pretended otherwise, but I didn't really have a choice."

She nodded. "Okay well, hurry up and change. We can share an Uber."

I frowned. "What's that, some kind of German energy drink?"

She closed her eyes, clearly embarrassed to know me. "It's an app people use to find rides. It's much faster and cheaper than using a taxi."

I frowned. "So you find someone on the app and trust that they aren't going to murder you the second you get in the back of their car?"

"They're not random people. Most of them are just off-duty taxi drivers trying to make extra money."

Right. Because off-duty taxi drivers are the most trustworthy people in the world.

"Sure, sounds good. On a totally unrelated note, do you think mace would fit in this clutch?"

• • •

When I stepped into Provisions the morning of my first team meeting, my heels echoed around the restaurant, announcing my presence to the unmanned hostess stand.

The lights were half dimmed overhead and the empty dining room was quiet, save for the morning crew working to make the restaurant spotless.

I took the long way around the courtyard, admiring the trees, and then stepped into the hallway that led toward the back offices. I was only two steps in when voices spilled out into the hallway from the back manager's office.

"Wait, wait, wait. She actually agreed to take the job?" a woman asked.

"Why wouldn't she? It's a great opportunity," Dean replied. Obviously, I quickly pressed against the sidewall and listened.

"Well yeah that would be enough for anyone else, but not for someone that you've been such a dick to. Let me guess, you mentioned the fact that you have a mega boner for her?"

"Zoe, cut that shit out. I mean it."

Zoe, the Provisions manager who'd hired me for my one and only shift tending bar.

"Yeah, you're right, wouldn't want her to know that you actually have a wittle baby grinch heart beneath that scrooge suit."

"If I wanted to show someone my heart, I'd adopt a puppy."

She grunted. "The idea of you with a dog is too scary to imagine."

"Lost?"

I nearly jumped out of my skin when a voice spoke directly behind me. I'd been so focused on eavesdropping that I hadn't noticed Julian until he was right behind me.

"Christ, Julian! Maybe announce yourself next time."

He smirked. "LILY, IT IS I, JULIAN," he boomed.

I narrowed my eyes. "Clever. Really clever."

I caught movement out of the corner of my eye and turned to see Zoe leaning out of the manager's office.

"Get in here you two," she said.

One look at her and Julian proved that I was one hundred percent overdressed for my first day on the job. Julian was in jeans and a button-down and Zoe was in white distressed overalls with a silky purple tank top underneath. Her colorful tattoos were on full display and she had a gold decorative ring adorning each one of her fingers. She looked like an Olsen twin, and I looked like a stuffy corporate lawyer in comparison.

"After you," Julian said, extending his arm for me to lead the way. "Good morning so far?"

I nodded. "Your girlfriend had to teach me how to use Uber."

He laughed. "Did she tell you that she used to think it was a dating app?"

"As fun as it is to listen to you two out there, we were supposed to start this meeting five minutes ago," Dean called from his office.

Julian arched a brow and I tried my best to suppress my laughter.

"I hate to say it, but I doubt either of us will win employee of the month now," I whispered.

"Damn. I really wanted that parking spot and a bad picture up on the wall," Julian said with a wink.

His comment pushed me over the edge. I lost it to a fit of laughter just as we rounded the corner into Dean's office. I was mid-laugh with my mouth open, clutching my chest, when my eyes locked on Dean. His sharp features were locked in a scowl, proving even further that the man was a walking time bomb.

His dark eyes followed me into his office and I

swallowed down the last bit of my laughter. Whatever humor I'd felt only moments before had been sucked away by Mr. Tightass. Did he ever relax?

CHAPTER FIFTEEN

DEAN

I'D BEEN IN a great mood that morning. After a seven mile run and a hot shower, I'd dressed in my favorite black suit. My white shirt was pressed and wrinkle free, and my shoes were shined to perfection. I'd had everything in control until I'd arrived at Provisions and Zoe had started in on the Lily crap again. She thought she was funny, but I needed every ounce of patience if I hoped to deal with Lily in a professional manner. Unfortunately, Zoe had worked me up just as Lily had arrived at the door of my office in a flirty blue dress, laughing at whatever joke Julian had just whispered to her.

The moment I saw her, adrenaline spiked my veins like my body was preparing for battle. My heart raced and I started to sweat. It wasn't a reaction I was used to, and as a result, I was reacting the worst way possible: with anger.

"Take a seat," I said, motioning to the four vacant chairs

spread out in front of my desk. Four open chairs, and Lily took the one closest to mine. Her perfume was soft and floral, a scent that lingered in the air between us.

"Are we waiting on someone else?" Julian asked, drawing my attention to him for the first time since he'd walked into the office. Lily had completely eclipsed his entrance.

"Hunter," I said.

Lily opened her mouth, but I knew what she was about to ask. "Hunter and Zoe have helped me with my last ten restaurants. The two veterans, along with fresh insight from you and Julian should make us a well-rounded team."

"What exactly is Hunter's role?" Julian asked, taking the open seat beside Lily. Zoe sat across from Lily, leaving the chair next to the door open for Hunter, whenever he finally arrived.

"He'll help find a location for the restaurant, and then I'll have him wear the hat of project manager during the build out."

"So will he—"

Lily's question was cut off by Hunter as he hurried into the office with sweat coating his brow.

"Sorry, sorry, sorry!" he announced, hands up in surrender. "I couldn't find a parking spot anywhere." His eyes cut around the room, taking in the two new members of the team. Julian garnered a quick onceover, but his eyes nearly fell out of his skull when he saw Lily.

"Oh shit, I didn't think you'd already be starting. Who are the newbies?"

Lily and Julian exchanged a glance before standing to greet Hunter.

"Julian Lefray, nice to meet you." I watched them exchange a handshake and Hunter nodded, clearly recognizing the name.

"Right, Mr. Moneybags. Good to have you here, man."

His hand dropped back to his side and then he turned toward Lily. His merino jacket could hardly button over his beer belly. The material strained as he bent forward for her hand, nearly breaking it off with his gusto.

"And who, may I ask, are you?"

Lily bristled at his veiled attempt at flirting. "Lily Black."

"She's the consultant I hired to help round out the food and drink menus, concept, and ambiance," I spoke up, if only to get the show on the road. "This was all in yesterday's email, Hunter. Now have a seat, we're already running behind."

His round cheeks reddened at my reprimand—that, or he was overheated from hustling to the meeting.

"Today won't take long. We need to check schedules and confirm a good time for our weekly meetings. I'd also like to finalize a name for the restaurant—"

Lily frowned. "I'm sorry, could we rewind a bit? You haven't even told me your vision for the restaurant yet. How am I supposed to help with a name if I don't even know what type of food we're serving?"

Fair enough. I leaned back in my chair. "I want to do a tapas bar with price points around fifteen dollars a dish."

"Accessible prices by New York standards," Zoe cut in.

Lily narrowed her eyes. "All right. Have you thought about whether this city really needs another tapas bar? Are you going to make it unique? Bring in flavors that separate us from other Spanish restaurants?" She didn't bother letting me answer before continuing. "I think it should have an old-world feel to it with options for paella on the menu for those that want bigger serving sizes."

She'd been there five minutes.

Five minutes and she was already giving me a headache.

What in the world had possessed me to hire her for this project?

"Lily, why don't you let me explain the entire concept before you start offering ideas? This meeting won't take long if you just listen for a few minutes."

Her jaw dropped and her bright eyes narrowed on me. I'd called her out in front of everyone, but she deserved it. She was a consultant. I was the boss.

"By all means, take it away."

Julian whispered something to her, and she smiled. Another private joke at my expense. Why was it so infuriating that Julian made her smile? Because it was at my expense?

Or because I wanted to switch places with him?

CHAPTER SIXTEEN

LILY

I MOVED INTO down dog and definitely felt my leg pop out of socket, like an overworked hand-me-down Barbie doll.

"Shit. I'm going down," I hissed, slowly sliding down onto my borrowed yoga mat until my face made contact with the sweaty rubber.

Josephine glanced over at me, sweat slipping down her face. She picked up her hand to flick it off, but it was no use. We were in a heated yoga class. The thermostat read 98 degrees and we were both going to die a slow death. The last sight I was going to see was the ass of the old hippie directly in front of me.

Did he have to wear the bike shorts?

Did they have to ride up *so* high?

"You're not supposed to just lay there," Josephine whispered.

The instructor told us to root down through our chakras and become one with the earth as we moved into our next round of sun salutations. I wanted to salute the sun with my middle finger.

"Lily. Come on! We can't go get crêpes after this if you don't work out." Josephine pushed to downward dog and then hopped to the front of her mat. My eyes followed her movements, but my body had no intention of getting up.

"Class! Class! I want you all to take a breath and look toward this student," the instructor said, *sounding dangerously close.* I glanced up to find her bulbous eyes hovering over me, hands motioning toward where I lay on my mat, face down, ass in the air. I'd quite literally collapsed in a heap of skin and bones. "Do you see how she listens to her body? She's taking this opportunity to do child's pose. While others push themselves toward unattainable goals, this student has set her own intentions for her practice today. I commend your work today, child."

HAHAHA. I was getting a gold star for being lazy.

I sent a gloating smile toward Josephine as Old Hippie started clapping, and soon the other students were joining in.

I'd officially won at yoga.

After class, I wiped down my body with my towel and then sprayed down my mat. *They'd probably be better off just burning the thing, but whatever.* Josephine and I grabbed our sandals and slipped out of the class before we could get stuck talking to the instructor. She was cornering students by the door, asking them how their bodies had responded to her words.

"Go, go, go," I hissed, pushing Josephine through the doorway just in the nick of time.

She called out after us. "Oh, girls! Great work in class today. Don't forget to pick up some tea tree oi—"

"Oh my god, she's still talking to us," Josephine said,

reaching back for my hand and pulling me farther down the street. We picked up the pace and didn't slow down until we were a few blocks away from the studio.

"Why in the world did we just do that?" Josephine asked.

I peeled my tank top off my chest, away from where it was suction-cupped to my skin with sweat. The fresh morning air was *much* better than the temperature of the yoga studio.

"Josephine, you just don't get it. Yoga is about far more than just exercise. For people like me—y'know *experienced* yogis—it's a way of life."

"Oh really? Name one yoga pose." She challenged me with an arched brow.

"Easy. Upper…moonbeam."

"No." She shook her head. "You're an idiot."

"Fine. Downward Dumbledore."

"There are no yoga poses named after Harry Potter characters."

I frowned. "Are you sure?"

She wrapped her sticky arm around my shoulder and pulled me in close. "Let's agree to never go back."

I nodded. "Never."

"Maybe we can pick up cycling or something?"

I groaned. "Can't we just be like those French women that stay skinny by walking a lot and doing the cayenne pepper cleanse?"

"You realize that when people do that cleanse, they don't eat or drink anything but juice for days?"

I stopped walking. "Oh god no. I thought you drank that crap *on top* of eating whatever you wanted."

"Yeah, Lily. 'Cause that's how diets work."

I shook my head. "Okay listen, let's go eat some crêpes,

and then tomorrow we'll worry about the long-term effects of eating a pastry full of Nutella."

She pulled the door open to the crêperie and ushered me inside. "Deal."

The inside of the shop smelled like a funnel cake had exploded. Small French-inspired tables were set up on either side of the center aisle and as we passed by the other patrons, I assessed their crêpe choices. There were savory ones with eggs and bacon, and sweet ones with fruit and chocolate sauces. One woman had a crêpe piled high with cinnamon apples and my hand actually itched to steal it from her.

The line to order was five people long, so we browsed the menus as we waited. *I want one of everything.*

"So how was the first day on the job? Was it nice having Julian there as your moral support?"

I bristled at the reminder of work. I'd barely managed to survive the meeting the day before, what with Dictator Dean stomping around like he owned the place. I mean, he did in fact own the place, but did he have to act like it *all* the time?

"It was okay. I met the rest of the team I'll be working with."

"Oh? Who else was there?"

"Zoe, the manager I told you about from my first night at Provisions. She's super awesome."

Josephine nodded.

"And then this guy named Hunter who gave off major creeper vibes the entire meeting."

Her eyes widened. "Why?"

"He was just *so* smarmy, like a New Jersey car salesman or something. He was covered in sweat when he got there and his suit barely fit over his beer belly. He gave me this flirty smile when I introduced myself to him, completely ignoring the big fat wedding ring on his left hand."

"Oh, gross."

I nodded. "Yeah. I was prepared to give him the benefit of the doubt, but then he asked if I wanted to get lunch with him, *alone*, after the meeting."

Her eyes widened. "What?!"

"I know."

"What'd you say?"

I shook my head. "Nothing. Dean called him back into the office before I could respond."

The customers in front of us finished ordering and we moved up to the front of the line.

"Hi, is this your first time to Uptown Crêperie?" asked the chipper cashier behind the cash register.

"Yes, but I'm not new to crêpes. I'd like a smores crêpe, a truffled caprese crêpe, and one of the apple cinnamon crème brûlée crêpes."

"Lily!" Josephine laughed. "That's enough food for an army."

"What? I'm going to review it all for my blog. I swear!"

"*Uh huh*. I use that same logic when I want to splurge on a Rebecca Minkoff purse."

I swiped my card and signed the receipt, already excited to take photos of the crêpes for my next blog post. I hadn't done a review of a crêperie in New York yet.

"Are we at least going to share those?" Josephine asked.

I glanced over at her with narrowed eyes. "Jo, I love you. I really do, but if you touch my crêpes, I'm gonna have to stab you with my fork."

CHAPTER SEVENTEEN

LILY

I CONSIDER MYSELF a decent person. I never steal candy from the bulk bins at the grocery store, I always bus my table at restaurants where it's clear that you're meant to, and I always let old people have my seat on the subway when it's full. (Okay maybe I just got elbowed out of my seat by a gruff grandma in the Bronx, but I'm counting it.) All of those good deeds didn't help the fact that I was about to become a murderer.

It was inevitable.

"You're not listening to me!" I said. "Here are all the reasons that the restaurant should have a Spanish name."

Dean wiped his hand down his face, clearly tired of arguing with me. We were back in his office, all five team members crammed into a space that seemed to be getting smaller by the minute.

Julian fidgeted in his seat, angling his body ever so slightly away from where I stood. Zoe leaned against the doorframe, watching Dean and I go at it with a little smile across her lips. Hunter hadn't spoken in the last fifteen minutes; he was too busy scrolling through his phone. The little trackball on his Blackberry made a ticking sound every time his finger scrolled over it and I was five seconds away from grabbing his phone and throwing it across the room.

"Lily. Do you know why my restaurants are successful?" Dean asked, leaning forward across his desk.

I rolled my eyes and threw my hands up in the air. "I would say dumb luck, but I have a feeling it's probably thanks to Zoe."

"Knucks," said Zoe, holding out her fist for me to pound.

He ignored my sarcasm. "It's because I control every single detail, from the menu prices down to the nails they use during construction."

I arched a brow. "That style of leadership only works when you're infallible, and last time I checked, you're not a god. You have to be able to recognize when other people just know better than you."

"Excuse me?" he asked, his brows furrowing in disbelief. Had anyone ever talked to him the way I did? How could they *not*?

"No one likes a tyrant! Especially one who is so stuck in his ways that he doesn't even realize a good idea when it's right in front of him."

He rubbed his hand over his mouth, probably trying to keep the curse words from spilling out. I was being harsh, unprofessional, and rude. Unfortunately, it was the only way I could get a word in edgewise with him. He'd blow right over me if I didn't speak up.

"Let's reiterate the roles really quickly," Dean said,

pointing to me. "You are here to help me with the food, drinks, and ambiance. End of story." He pointed to himself. "I will handle every other detail of the restaurant, including the name."

I crossed my arms, feeling my face flush with anger.

Sorry Mom.

You raised a murderer.

My eyes glanced over his desk for a sharp instrument to stick in his black-hole-of-a-heart, but there was nothing save for an expensive pen clutched in his fist.

"You know what I think we need?" Zoe asked, pushing off the doorframe and circling back behind Dean's desk. Her head barely came up to his shoulders, but he still looked down in fear of what she was about to say. "Some team bonding."

Hunter grunted and Julian laughed. I stood in silence, waiting for Dean's reaction.

"C'mon," Zoe said. "Let's take your boat out this weekend and relax. No talk about the restaurant. Just fun."

"Josephine has been bugging me about going back out on the water," Julian added.

Before Dean could reject the plan, Zoe turned her gaze on me. "You in, Black?"

If I said yes, I'd look overly eager.

If I said no, I'd look like I was the asshole of the group.

I sighed, picked up my clipboard from the edge of Dean's desk, and then plopped down in my seat. "Yeah, whatever."

She clapped. "Perfect!"

"Saturday morning?" Julian asked, already pulling out his phone, undoubtedly Snapchatting his lover. *Blech.*

Dean offered Julian a curt nod, and just like that, the meeting was adjourned. We'd succeeded in making zero decisions, but I was marginally closer to losing my voice from yelling at Dean. That counted for something, I guess.

Julian stood to talk something over with Dean and Zoe in the hallway, and I reached down to grab my purse. A shadow loomed over me as I sat back up, and I realized too late that Hunter was practically on top of me as he leaned over my chair. His heavy cologne nearly choked me to death.

"Oh, wow, that's close," I mutter, leaning as far away from him as I could. The guy clearly didn't know the concept of personal space.

"Looking forward to seeing you out on the boat this weekend, Lily," he said, dropping his hand on the back of my chair.

"Oh, uh yeah, should be fun," I replied with a curt, pleasant smile.

"I'm glad we'll have some time to chat." He waggled his eyebrow. "Just you and me."

Oh my god. How was no one hearing this crap?

I narrowed my eyes up at him and pointed at where his hand sat on the back of my chair. His thin gold wedding band was two inches from my shoulder. "What kind of ring is that on your finger?" I asked, playing the not-so-subtle game of "fuck off".

He laughed.

"The *slippery* kind," he replied with a snakelike hiss.

I stood so abruptly that he had to flinch back to avoid my head colliding with his face. "You're disgusting."

"Aw, c'mon, can't you take a little joke?"

I brushed past him and stepped into the hallway. Dean, Zoe, and Julian stood in silence as I stepped past them. I knew they'd heard the last part of our conversation, but I didn't bother stopping to correct their assumptions. I headed toward the front of the restaurant and prayed there was a cab waiting for me. I was in a different town, but I was still dealing with the same old crap. Hunter saw blonde hair and tits. He didn't see me as a colleague.

"Hey! Jeez. Would you wait up a second?"

I heard Dean's voice, shocked that he cared enough to follow me out onto the sidewalk. His hand hit my forearm, inches from my palm, and I froze, surprised by the comfort of his grip.

"You said the meeting was over," I said, staring up at him for confirmation.

"It is."

I shrugged, shying away from his touch, but his hand tightened on my arm. "Well, I'm leaving then. I'll see you on Saturday."

"What did Hunter just do?" he asked, ignoring my brush off.

A part of me wanted to cover up Hunter's attempted indiscretion. I'd dealt with this situation plenty of times before. *A male superior came on to you? Did you tempt him in some way? Surely, you lead him on.*

"It wasn't a big deal. Hunter came on to me and I told him off. End of story."

He nodded and rolled his lips together as he mulled over how to proceed. "I'll take care of it."

I swallowed. He sounded like a mobster. Did he have brass knuckles hidden in a pocket of that designer suit? "What are you going to do?"

The edge of his lip curled up as he met my eyes. "Nothing that will leave scars."

My eyes widened. Oh shit.

"Lily, I'm joking. I'm not going to beat Hunter up because he hit on you."

I smirked. "Maybe just a little kick in the balls? Or a karate chop? Nothing major."

He rolled his eyes and dropped his hand. My arm felt instantly lighter, like it might float away without the weight of his hand holding it down.

"See you Saturday," he said, taking a step back. His eyes scanned over my face and across my cheeks. "Don't forget sunscreen."

I tilted my head and smiled. "Y'know if I didn't know any better, I'd think that you were being nice to me right now."

He smiled and then bent his head toward the ground to hide it. By the time he glanced back up, the smile was gone, but there was still humor in his eyes.

"Yeah? Well don't get used to it."

CHAPTER EIGHTEEN

DEAN

"SIR, EVERYTHING IS set. As soon as your guests arrive, I'm prepared to head out."

I nodded at the captain. "Sounds good."

"How long would you like to be out on the water?"

I thought of Lily, of how volatile she made me feel. "Let's make this a short trip. Just a few hours."

The less time I had to spend in close proximity to her, the better. Every minute I spent arguing with her probably shaved off another year of my life.

He nodded and then retreated back to the helm. I reclined on the sundeck's couch and took the opportunity to check my email one final time before everyone arrived.

I had the usual crap clogging up my inbox, but third from the top, there was an email I'd been waiting to receive for the last few days. I scrolled past the introduction and smiled.

Mr. Harper, I'd be happy to meet with you during LV Restaurant Week. I have available appointments throughout the event, so once you and your team know your schedule, get in touch with me and we can work something out. In the meantime, I'll start preparing dishes.

Las Vegas Restaurant Week was an annual event. For one week a year, every restaurateur worth their shit dropped everything and headed to Sin City. LVRW was where deals were brokered, chefs were hired, drinks were thought up, and new fads were invented. I'd been on the fence about attending again, but that email changed everything.

Antonio Acosta was the executive chef at the most famous tapas restaurant in Los Angeles. For a pretty penny, he was willing to advise me on the menu for the new restaurant and it was an opportunity I couldn't pass up.

I headed down into the en suite cabin to swap my phone out for my laptop. I needed to book last minute flights for my team and then try and scramble to find a hotel room.

"What a shocker!" Zoe said, stepping through the threshold wearing a black one-piece and jean shorts. She had a towel clutched under her arm and a bag slung over her shoulder. "You're out on your yacht and you're working."

I smiled and turned my computer around so she could see the airline's website. "No choice. We're going to LVRW."

Her jaw dropped. "What? I thought we were going to skip it this year."

I explained the recent change of events.

"Well shit," she said, dropping her towel and bag on the cabin's floor. "Everyone is up on the sundeck. I'll go fill them in."

"Call Hunter too," I yelled out as she set off for the stairs. "He's not coming today."

I turned back to my computer and scanned through the available rooms at the Bellagio. I knew it would be slim pickings. The hotel booked up quickly on a normal week, but the fact that it was also the home base for the convention ensured that we would be lucky if we found a room within a five-mile radius. I scanned through the availability for the guest rooms and suites, not shocked to find them all booked.

I was about to call the hotel to book one of their nine private villas, when I heard Lily's voice on the stairs.

"Does he think we have no life? I can't just drop everything and leave town on a moment's notice."

I rolled my eyes. "You will if you plan on getting paid this month," I yelled.

She came into view at the door of my suite, arms crossed over her short white cover-up. Her tan shoulders were bare and her bright red suit was just barely visible beneath the thin fabric of her dress. Her long legs were more on display than they'd ever been—a tempting sight that I didn't indulge in. Her blonde hair was tied back at the base of her neck, allowing me to take in every ounce of anger written across her features. She was pissed. I was intrigued.

"You can't force me to go to Vegas," she countered.

I smirked. "Antonio Acosta has agreed to help us with the menu for the new restaurant."

Her grip loosened on her arms. She knew that name. "Are you kidding me?"

I shook my head.

"When do we fly out?" she asked, her tone slightly less abrasive than before.

"Wednesday, assuming I can book this villa in time."

She swallowed and nodded. I could see the excitement growing behind her gaze. The Las Vegas Restaurant Week was an invite-only event. It was exclusive and elite. I knew how badly Lily wanted to attend, and I knew she would have admitted that desire to anyone but me.

Why?

Because we were both playing the same game.

"Julian said he's available up until Friday," Zoe explained, cutting her gaze between Lily and me. "He'll need to fly home before us."

I nodded. "As long as he's there for part of the week, it should be fine."

"And Hunter?" Lily asked, her gaze focused on Zoe.

"He'll be there, but he's been warned about his behavior. Don't worry."

She nodded, seeming to accept my answer.

Zoe clapped, breaking the silence. "Okay, well, we'll go mix some drinks on the deck and let you finish up. Let me know if you need my help with anything."

Zoe pulled Lily's arm and they turned toward the stairs. I focused on Lily's body as she walked away, wondering if it was a good idea to book one villa for all five team members. There'd be plenty of space for everyone, but something told me that staying in a hotel room—*even a large one*—with Lily Black would be temptation in its most extreme form.

● ● ●

By the time I'd finished booking everything, we'd dropped anchor in open ocean. I surfaced from my cabin, hot and cranky, and paused at the top of the stairs. Zoe was lounging on the sundeck with her sunglasses covering most of her face. Julian and Josephine were sitting on the couch beneath the roofed section of the sundeck. Julian leaned in and kissed her cheek. I looked away and my gaze followed the line of the sundeck until I spotted Lily behind my bar, wearing nothing but her red bikini and one of my old Nicks caps. It sat crooked on her head, the wide brim covering her entire forehead.

"Where'd you find that?" I asked, stepping closer.

A smarter man would have stepped in the opposite direction.

She glanced up and blanched. "It was in a cupboard down in the galley. I forgot a hat and I get so many freckles if I don't keep my cheeks covered in the sun."

I tilted my head, taking in her delicate features beneath the brim of my hat. She already had freckles across her cheeks, but I liked them.

"I can take it off."

I shook my head and bent down to retrieve a few limes from a bowl beneath the bar.

"Keep it on."

I purposely didn't look to see her reaction.

"What are you going to make?" she asked, taking a hesitant step closer.

She smelled like summer. That tropical scent that warms your stomach.

"A margarita," I said, peering at her from the corner of my eye.

Her red tube top style bikini was tight and had the effect of drawing me in like a moth to a flame.

"That's my favorite drink," she said, a small smile stretching across her lips.

I sliced up two limes, squeezed the juice into the shaker, and reached for the triple sec. "I usually like to use fresh orange juice, but this'll do."

I pulled the cork from my Patrón and poured in two shots. A little ice and a splash of agave nectar went in next, and then I shook the drink up while Lily watched me in silence.

"Try it," I said.

Her hand brushed mine as she took the glass from me. Lily brought the glass to her lips and took a small sip. Her bright eyes met mine over the brim of the glass and I knew I had her. She was a better bartender than I was, but I'd been perfecting margaritas since I was sixteen.

"It's good."

"You can keep it," I said, already reaching for two more limes.

"You're being nice again today," she quipped, pressing her hip against the bar to face me.

I shot her a dark look. "You won't be saying that in a few minutes."

She narrowed her eyes. "Why?"

"You'll find out as soon as you finish that drink."

CHAPTER NINETEEN

DEAN

DURING THE SUMMER months, when the sundeck is hot and the water is too tempting to ignore, I like to jump off the side of my yacht into the water. It isn't dangerous if you do it right, but when I broached the subject to the group, everyone but Julian reacted like I was insane.

"No!" Josephine yelled, leaning out over the edge of the railing. "That's how people get eaten by sharks."

"There are no sharks," I corrected her, reaching for the hem of my shirt. I tugged if off and tossed it back onto the floor of the main deck. When I turned back toward the railing, Lily was watching me. Her eyes dragged down my chest, heating my skin. I cleared my throat and she smirked, meeting my eye for only a moment before glancing away. She wasn't embarrassed to have been caught. She was too self-assured to be bothered by the fact that I knew she was checking me out.

"I think we should do it," Zoe said, tossing her

sunglasses aside. "It'll be a bonding exercise."

Lily grunted. "Will the bonding part come when we're all at the hospital nursing broken bones?"

I smiled and shook my head. She and Josephine would come around. Everyone did. "I've done it a million times."

Lily's wide eyes met mine. "It's that easy to do?"

Josephine slapped her palm against her forehead. "This is dumb. We shouldn't do this."

Zoe was ahead of everyone. She already had one leg swung over the metal rail, balanced on the short ledge that extended out a few inches on the other side. I stayed close until she swung her other leg over and had a solid grip on the railing.

Julian helped lift Josephine over the railing even as she continued to protest. "How confident are you about the sharks?"

He laughed off her question and then swung himself over the railing beside her. Zoe, Julian, and Josephine spread out along the side of the boat, a few feet apart. Lily stayed where she was, her feet firmly planted on the safe side of the rail.

"You going to chicken out?" I asked, stepping up behind her.

"I haven't decided yet," she replied, sliding her gaze back to me.

I smiled and reached up to take the hat off her head.

"Hey—I didn't say I was going to do it," she protested, trying in vain to flatten down her blonde hair. It was curly and wild from the salty air.

"There are no sharks," I assured her.

She narrowed her eyes on me. "Maybe it's not the sharks I'm scared of…"

"What then?" I asked.

She inhaled a breath and whipped around to face the railing. "Just hold on to me as I climb over."

I reached out and slid my hands around her slender waist. Her skin was so warm from the sun and I gripped her tight enough that even if she tripped, she wouldn't fall. The bottom of her bikini shifted, revealing a sliver of pale skin. I yearned to see more—to see the parts of her that the sun couldn't reach.

"Okay, I'm just going to swing my leg over…"

I nodded in response, knowing if I spoke my voice would likely reveal the attraction I was trying to keep hidden.

She stretched her left leg out over the rail and then twisted her body as if she were hopping over the top of a fence. I lifted her and kept her steady, and when she was on the opposite side, both feet on the platform, she glanced up at me. I could feel the adrenaline pumping through her veins. Our pulses were blending and for two seconds, I thought we'd kiss. Right there with everyone watching.

"You can let go now," she said, shifting her gaze from my lips up to my eyes.

I snapped back to reality like a rubber band, let go of her waist, and took two steps back. One step wouldn't have been enough. One step meant I could still lean forward and kiss her. Two steps gave me back my control.

"C'mon Dean! I'm jumping with or without you!" Zoe yelled.

I laughed and hopped the railing in one clean jump.

"Okay, jump on one," Julian yelled.

"Three."

I leveraged my body over the blueish green water and took a breath.

"Two!"

"Oh Jesus, this is stupid," Lily whispered next to me.

My heart raced as if it were trying to fight its way from my chest.

"One!" Julian yelled.

I bent my knees, reached out for Lily's hand, and pulled her off the ledge with me.

She let out a wild scream as we flew through the air. The water rushed to meet us and I held my breath just before we crashed through the surface. The cold water overtook us and I let go of Lily's hand so I could kick back to the surface. Endorphins spiked my blood, mixing with the adrenaline from the few seconds of flight. I'd taken that jump hundreds of times, but never while connected to someone else.

I broke the surface and inhaled a deep breath. Julian and Josephine were already kicking back to the dive ladders, and Zoe was climbing onto the swim platform. Lily was nowhere to be found.

I spun in a circle, cursing the fact that we were swimming off the shore of New York and not in the Caribbean. The water was too dark to see below the surface, and for two seconds I feared I wouldn't be able to find her if she'd hurt herself during the jump. I sucked in a deep breath, preparing to go back down to search for her, just as her blonde hair broke the surface. She coughed up water and pushed her hair back out of her face, out of sorts, but seemingly uninjured.

"Are you okay?" I asked, paddling closer.

Her wide eyes turned to me and she held out one hand, using the other to tread water.

"Do. Not. Come. Any. Closer." She enunciated each word as if she'd chop my head off if I didn't heed her warning.

"What's wrong?"

I paddled closer and her eyes flared with warning.

"DEAN. Do not come any closer."

That's when I noticed what she was trying desperately to hide.

Oh shit.

"My top came off when I hit the water."

She scanned the water around her, frantic. And me?

I tried my damnedest to keep the smirk off my face.

CHAPTER TWENTY

LILY

"EVERYONE TURN AROUND!" I yelled. "SO HELP ME GOD!"

Julian helped pull Jo up out of the water and she collapsed into a fit of laughter on the swim platform. Julian covered his eyes with one hand and bent down to pull her up with the other.

"I can't see anything! I swear. I'm just going to go back into the galley."

Josephine kept howling with laughter, unable to even catch her breath. I'd kill her as soon as I found my bathing suit top. Hell, maybe I'd just strangle her with it.

Zoe was currently the only person on my good side. As far as I was concerned, Jo was dead to me. Her and Dean, both. When I turned back around, he was still treading water a few feet away from me, completely unfazed by my death threats.

"I hate you."

He tilted his head and a little smirk stretched across his

lips. "I can't see anything."

"You're lying," I said, glancing down to confirm my boobs were below the surface. Every time the ocean current bobbed me up and down, I feared one would pop out, much to Dean's delight.

He shook his head. "There's no use looking for your top. You're going to drown trying to find it."

I groaned and glanced back to the boat. "Josephine! Jo! Will you stop laughing for two seconds and help me?"

She was absolutely no use. "Lily." She breathed through laughter. "I'll help, just let me—" She couldn't even get the sentence out without erupting into another fit of cackling.

The burning sensation in my arms was becoming harder to ignore; I couldn't tread water for much longer.

"Josephine! This isn't funny! Some shark is probably smelling my bikini top and deciding he wants to eat me for lunch!"

Dean groaned. "For the last time, there are *no* sharks."

I turned back around and...GOD DAMN HIM. He was closer than ever. I didn't have a choice. I had to swim to the boat and get out without my bikini top. Josephine wasn't going to get off her bony butt and help me. Either I succumbed to my fate and drowned, or I got out and let Dean see my life-changing rack, thus ruining him for all future women from there on out. (Okay, maybe I was hyping myself up a *little* bit.)

I started paddling back to the boat, already breathing heavily from having to tread water for so long. Dean swam right past me, reached the ladder, and pulled himself up and out, all before I even got close to the boat. *Show off.* His tan, smooth chest glistened in the sun as he bent back down for my hand.

"I can get out myself," I said, covering my chest with

one arm and using the other arm to doggy paddle closer to the ladder. It was slow going, but I figured I'd get there eventually.

"The ladder isn't stable. Stop being difficult and just let me help you," he argued.

Me? DIFFICULT? So help me god, he was going to eat his words when I got onto that platform.

"I have strong arms. Turn around and let me get up."

"Lily. Enough."

The fire in my veins had nothing to do with treading water and everything to do with my anger toward Dean. I was right against the ladder, just below where he was hovering on the platform. I had one arm wrapped precariously around my chest and one arm desperately trying to keep me afloat...which left me with zero arms to reach for the ladder. *Fuck me.*

I had to suck it up and wait him out. Eventually he'd get bored and go inside, and I could lift myself out then. The muscles in my arm started cramping worse than ever, like they'd heard my thoughts and were desperately trying to convince me to abort my plan. My pain must have shown on my face because Dean bent lower, too annoyed to deal with my nonsense any longer.

"Lily, I'm going to help you up. You can yell all you want, but I'm not going to let you kill yourself because you're afraid I'll see your boobs."

I tried to reach for the ladder with my swimming arm just as I felt his hands grasp my biceps. He yanked my arm away from where it covered my chest and hoisted me out of the water like he was lifting a bag of marshmallows. I didn't even have time to fully comprehend the fact that my boobs were on full display before I felt one foot touch the edge of the platform.

I was on land again!

I wasn't going to die!

Unfortunately, excitement set in a moment too soon. Just as I tried to set my other foot down on the platform, it slipped out from under me. Dean tried to hold me up, but I was already flailing forward like a fish. I couldn't brace myself against him because he still had ahold of my arms. I fell in slow motion, confident my face was about to make contact with the hard platform, when instead, I landed face first against Dean's crotch.

Wait. Let me clarify.

I'd been on the edge of the swim platform with Dean holding me up like a rag doll, and when I slipped, my face had hit his crotch with enough force to strip the paint off his bow, *if you catch my drift.* I was pretty sure I'd just broken Dean's penis. *Hello God? It's me, Lily. If it wouldn't be too much trouble, could you have a shark jump out of the water and eat me? I'd really like to die a quick, painless death, preferably one that doesn't involve my face colliding with Dean's crotch any more.*

Dean let out a guttural grown, let go of my arms, and collapsed back onto the swim platform. He squeezed his eyes shut and rocked from side to side with bent knees. I jumped up and leaned over him, gripping his shoulders in my hands.

"Oh my god. I'm so sorry! I'm so sorry!"

One of his eyes peered open and he shook his head, incapable of speech. Clearly, I'd just caused some serious damage.

"Do you need some ice? Should I blow on it?"

He laughed, and then groaned again. The joke was crass at best, but I needed a way to gauge how badly he was injured.

"Okay good, if you can laugh then you aren't going to die."

I heard footsteps on the stairs and glanced up to see Josephine, taking them two at a time. With all the excitement, I hadn't even noticed that she'd left the swim platform. "I've got it! Here, Lily, I've got something for you to wear!"

I glanced down to my chest, remembered it was bare, and then jumped off Dean. Jeez, I'd just played the role of slutty nurse really well. *Oh please, let me help you while I shove my boobs in your face.*

"You perv! You could have reminded me that I was topless," I said, holding my arms over my chest.

Dean opened his eyes and glared up at me. "Yeah, sorry, I was a little busy trying not to throw up from pain."

Josephine thrust a bright red thing in front of my face. "Here, put this on."

A normal person would have grabbed a t-shirt or a towel. What did Josephine grab? A giant, puffy life vest— the kind you find on cheap paddleboats. It would cover my boobs, but only barely.

"Seriously Jo? Seriously?"

She glared at me, holding it out for me to take. "What?! It was the only thing I could find. Just put it on."

I huffed and took it from her. It wouldn't cover me completely, but it was better than nothing. I turned away from Dean and quickly pulled it on over my head. I buckled it in front of my chest and tightened the black strap as tight as it would go. By the time I turned back around, Dean was staring up at me with a blank expression.

"What?" I asked, glancing down to confirm that the life vest was covering me.

Josephine laughed. "He's probably just recalling all of

his boyhood Playboy fantasies."

He shook his head and pushed up to stand. He towered over me, tall and lean. I could smell the ocean air mixed with his body wash.

"More like Baywatch," he corrected with a little smirk.

I groaned with embarrassment. "Could we just pretend that you didn't see any of that?" I pleaded.

He arched a brow and met my eye. There was an emotion concealed behind his gaze that I hadn't seen before, at least not from him.

"Not possible," he said, shaking his head. I watched him take the stairs back up to the deck and realized that the tension brewing between the two of us wasn't gone. Our time together on the boat had morphed it into something much harder to control...

CHAPTER TWENTY-ONE

LILY

AFTER THE BOAT ride from hell, I knew it'd be hard to face Dean at work. I stayed in bed late on Sunday, trying to recreate my memory of the events from the day before. Sometimes I could convince myself that I'd looked cool and sexy with my life preserver on, and then other times my brain replayed the moment when my face collided with Dean's crotch over and over again like a perfectly looped video that never seemed to end.

When I checked my email that night and saw Dean's name, I half expected the subject line to read "Obviously, You're Fired."

From: Dean Harper
To: Lily Black, Julian Lefray, Zoe Davis, Hunter Smith
Subject: LVRW

As you know, we have a very busy week coming up. We leave for LVRW on Wednesday so I'd like to have a meeting at my house tomorrow morning. We'll go over the flight, accommodations, and our schedules for the few days we'll be in Vegas.

My address is below. We'll start at 9:30 AM.

D. Harper

Huh. No mention of how his crotch-el region was healing up. I'd take that as a good sign.

● ● ●

I stood on Dean's doorstep and knocked, but no one answered. I rang the doorbell, but it felt useless. His front door was black, shiny, and solid. There were no windows to peer through, and the windows along the foyer were dark.

I spun in a circle, trying to decide if I was at the correct house. His Upper West Side townhouse was tucked in a row of stately brownstones. Down the block, I'd passed a neighborhood deli with trendy French tables and ivy vines that looked like they'd been growing for the last hundred years. I'd almost stopped inside for a latte, but I hadn't wanted to run late. Now, however, it seemed the latte would have been useful. I yawned and tried to cover it, telling myself I wasn't actually as tired as I felt. Sleep had been elusive the last two nights. I'd filled my days with work, but at night, when my head hit my pillow and I had a moment alone with my thoughts, I'd replay my encounters with Dean.

The way we fought, the way he infuriated me, the way he intrigued me. I couldn't decide where he fit in my mind's Venn diagram. On the left side, I had people I hated, and on the right, I had the people I loved. Right in the middle, in a category of his own making, there was Dean Harper.

I tried the doorbell for the second time and then reached for the door handle. It was unlocked. I pushed the door open and stepped into his foyer.

"Hello?"

I took a tentative step forward and spoke up. "Dean?"

My shoes echoed across the black-and-white marble floor. His house, from what I could see, was immaculate and designed to a T. The entryway was a round circular room with a black chandelier hanging above a black lacquered table. There were formal elements, like the chandelier and crown molding, interspersed with masculine details. His bike hung in the hallway leading from the entryway to a large, hand-carved staircase. Photos hung on the wall around the entryway; blown-up versions of Dean as a baby drew me closer.

I slipped off my heels—I figured Dean probably had a no-shoes-in-the-house policy—and stepped closer to the first photo to my left. Dean was young, maybe one or two, sitting on a rocking horse wearing a diaper, cowboy boots, and a cowboy hat. His chubby belly made me smile as I moved on to the next photo. Dean was older in that one, with buckteeth and a choppy bowl cut. His blond hair was bright, almost white, and he had popsicle juice streaked across his face as he sat beside an old man on a tractor. The old man was waving at the camera, but Dean was looking up at him, enamored.

I scanned through the rest of the photos on the wall,

taking in Dean with braces and Dean on the day he graduated from college, surrounded by his loved ones. I circled back to the table at the entry, too intimidated to venture into any of the other rooms on the first floor. There was a pile of mail on the table, mostly boring envelopes with bills, and catalogs he'd yet to recycle, but stacked on the very top, there was a colorful postcard with a picture of a massive cave beneath the words "Maquoketa Caves State Park". I glanced up the stairs, listened for footsteps, and then turned the postcard over.

"Dean,

I know you just visited, but I couldn't resist sending you a post card from your favorite park. I got your dad to go down into the cave earlier. He pretended to hate it, but I know he had fun. Maybe the next time you visit we can come back and camp here like old times.

Love you,
Mom"

"Is it a Texan custom to break into your friends' houses and rifle through their mail?"

I swallowed and glanced up to see Dean standing at the top of the stairs. His jaw was clean-shaven and his hair had pomade in it, momentarily coaxing the wavy strands into submission. His red tie sat in the center of his pressed white shirt and his navy suit fit him like a glove. He looked like he had the entire world under his thumb...beginning with me.

"I rang your doorbell," I explained with a shaky voice.

He started down the stairs, dragging his hand along the smooth rail. His dark eyes stayed on me.

"And then I called your name."

He arched an eyebrow, but stayed silent.

"Your door was unlocked," I said, pointing to it as if it would speak up and confirm my story.

He stepped from the stairs down onto the marble floor, dragging his eyes up over my outfit. I glanced down. My dress was black and slimming with a sweetheart neckline. I'd stuffed a cardigan in my tote with plans to put it on before I'd arrived. Without it, the dress was a little too risqué for work. There was too much skin exposed across my neck and chest if Hunter was going to be around.

"The meeting doesn't start until 9:30. I was showering," he explained, drawing my attention back up to him.

I reached for the cream cardigan. His gaze followed the fabric as I pulled it on over my shoulders. "Then I guess I read your email wrong."

He knocked his knuckles against the table twice and then stepped back. "C'mon. We'll wait for the others in the kitchen. I need some coffee."

I trailed after him, focusing on the black hardwood floors that began just off the entryway. We passed his bicycle hanging on the wall like a modern art installation and then turned the corner into the kitchen, just to the left of the main staircase. The dark wood floors extended into the room, but they were balanced out with light gray cabinets and Carrera marble countertops. Every gadget I dreamed of having in my future kitchen was on full display inside Dean's. A restaurant-grade refrigerator sat beside a built-in espresso maker and I swear to god, my heart fluttered a little bit at the sight of the black KitchenAid mixer.

"Espresso?" he asked,

I scrunched my nose. "Latte?"

He nodded as I moved around the large island, giving

him space to move. There seemed to be no limit to his talents. Bartender, barista, yachtsman, restaurateur—the talent had to end somewhere, right? *Probably in the bedroom.*

I slid a barstool out from beneath the island and sat as I watched him work, letting my question take root in my mind. Dean had all the things that a good lover was supposed to have. He moved and spoke with utter confidence. He had a killer body from working out, which would also help with stamina in the bedroom. He bent to see into the back of his refrigerator and I smiled at his ass. *Yet another bonus.*

Experience in the bedroom mattered as well, but that wasn't something I could find out from looking at him.

"Do you go on a lot of dates, Dean?" I asked, letting my thoughts seep out into the open before I could stop them.

He glanced away from his refrigerator. A navy-clad shoulder gave way to smirking lips and curious eyes.

"Will I have to write you up alongside Hunter for sexual harassment?"

I laughed. "That question was hardly *harassment*."

He pulled the carton of milk from his refrigerator and set it down on the island in front of me, precisely and thoughtfully. I could see the veins in his hands, evidence of an early morning workout, no doubt.

"It's not like you have to prove anything to me," I continued. "I was just wondering…"

I let the second half of the sentence linger, suddenly feeling too nervous to expand on my thoughts.

"Wondering what?"

His eyes dared me to be honest, and I'd never been good at turning down a dare.

"It just seems like guys like *you*—the powerful assholes

of the world—are supposed to be really good in bed." His eyes widened only slightly, and I swore I saw the muscles in his jaw tighten. He propped his hands up on the edge of the island and leaned forward, gaze locked on mine.

"And what has your experience been?"

I shook my head. "I've only been with guys my own age."

"So?"

I shrugged. "In college, anyone can be a rich kid, with a big ego and daddy's checkbook. It's another thing entirely to be powerful on your own."

His nostrils flared and then he pushed back off the counter. "Well if you ever care to put your little theory to the test, you know where to find me."

I laughed.

He was joking.

He *had* to be joking.

Right?

I opened my mouth to clarify but the doorbell rang before I could. Loud, obnoxious, and horribly timed.

CHAPTER TWENTY-TWO

DEAN

I ROUNDED THE corner back to my house, but instead of slowing down, I passed my stoop and kept going. My run was over, but the fire inside of me wasn't tamed. My problem with Lily was no closer to be solved.

The meeting at my house the day before had gone to shit within the first five minutes. The team had gathered around my kitchen so we could go over final items for Vegas, but the entire time, I could feel Lily's curious gaze on me. She'd sat at my kitchen table, picking apart my words in her mind and making them out to be more than they'd been. The dare I'd spoken just before everyone had arrived had been a joke. Nothing more. I could have clarified that, but instead, I'd let it linger between us, suffocating the room with questions.

I could still reach out to her and squash the invitation. I had her email, her cell phone number, and her address, but something held me back.

It was that *something* that made me want to keep running.

CHAPTER TWENTY-THREE

LILY

I STOOD ACROSS the street from Dean's house, knowing full well that I shouldn't have been standing across the street from Dean's house. It was the night before we were supposed to leave for Vegas. I had a flight at 8 AM, a few things left to pack, and at least another hundred reasons why I shouldn't have been staring at Dean's black lacquered front door.

All day, I'd replayed his words in my mind. All day, I'd backtracked and broken down and read between the lines. I ran through Central Park with my iPod blaring and still, Dean's words rang louder. I stood in line at a coffee shop and tried to find a single guy that was as attractive as Dean. As annoying. As bossy. As *challenging*. I ate at a newly opened deli for lunch, hoping to review it for my blog, but I'd finished off my sandwich without registering a single flavor.

Dean had me wrapped up around him with a single sentence.

"Well if you ever care to put your little theory to the test, you know where to find me."

Fuck him.

I pulled my phone out of my purse and texted Jo.

Lily: I'm about to have sex in New York for the first time...

Jo: Whoa! Please say it's not going to be with Hobo Nelson.

Lily: Dean.

Jo: Wait. Wait. Wait. ABORT. Answer your phone.

She called right then, illuminating my screen with her photo. I ignored her. I wasn't looking for her blessing; I just wanted her to know where to find me in case Dean and I accidentally killed each other.

I slipped my phone back into my purse as it continued to ring. Phone call. Voicemail. Phone call. Voicemail. Jo wouldn't stop until I picked up. Instead, I took my first step across the street as my heart started to thump in my chest, too hard to go unnoticed. The lights were off in his house. For all I knew, he wasn't home.

Still, I had to try.

In an out-of-body experience, I watched my heels ascend to the top of his stoop, and then I was on his doorstep and I had nowhere to go but forward. I reached out and rang his doorbell. I could hear it chime inside, echoing across his marble floors. My stomach dipped and *suddenly* I felt sick and *suddenly* I wasn't sure this was such a good idea. I clutched my stomach. My phone kept vibrating with Josephine's warnings and I felt like I was going to throw up.

I took a step back, prepared to bolt. My throat felt tight

and my legs felt weak. I just needed to get off his stoop and then I could sit and breathe and berate myself for being so monumentally stupid. And then his door opened slowly, and Dean was standing there in the dim light of his house, and I was absolutely in over my head.

He didn't say a word, just stood there shirtless, tan, and surprised to see me. His black drawstring pants were loose, holding on to his hips and defying the law of gravity. I could see a sliver of his Calvin Klein underwear just below a razor-edged Adonis V that cut into his abs so hard it looked almost painful. His hair was wavy and unruly, just like mine...and *suddenly* I didn't feel sick and *suddenly* I was sure this was a good idea.

"Lily?"

He spoke my name like it was a question. I knew the answer.

I shook my head and stepped forward, pressing my hands to his chest and pushing him back into his house. His hands found my hips. He gripped my workout top and scrunched the material in his palms so he could feel my skin underneath. I hadn't even thought to change before coming over; I was a mess, sweaty from my workout and running around the city all day. My running tights were stained with coffee and I would have showered had I even thought I might actually be there, standing in front of Dean and accepting his challenge.

There were two seconds where I had control. I'd taken him by surprise by showing up at his doorstep, but he recovered quickly, pulling me deeper into his house and making it that much harder to second-guess my decision.

"Well if you ever care to put your little theory to the test, you know where to find me."

CHAPTER TWENTY-FOUR

DEAN

I KNEW THIS would happen. I knew that by playing with Lily, by testing her and teasing her, eventually she would bite back. Her bite wasn't painful. It was a naughty dream that bled into waking hours. Her tank top and leggings were stretched across her skin so that I could see every curve that lay hidden beneath.

The second her hands hit my chest, I knew what she wanted. I'd truly been half-joking the day before, but I should have known Lily would accept a half-thrown gauntlet. She was a feisty little twenty-something. She thought she knew the world and she thought she could show up on a man's doorstep late at night. *So fucking naive.*

She dragged her nails down my chest and I grabbed her hips, squeezing through the thin material. We could make it up to my room, but that was half a world away, and I needed her right there. In the foyer, on the cold marble.

I kicked the door closed and yanked off her black tank top. Her wide, bright eyes were the size of saucers. Her lips were plump and pink. We hadn't even kissed yet, but by the morning, those lips would be red and swollen. She'd have to put ChapStick on them for two days straight and every time she did, she'd remember when I'd bent down and stolen that first kiss, gripping her hips and yanking her toward me.

When our mouths connected, she groaned, and I ground her hips against mine. Her tongue slipped past my lips and I tilted my head, bringing her closer. She tasted good, like cinnamon gum. I smiled. She'd planned this. She'd chewed gum on the way over. She'd thought of me all day. She wanted me to slip my hand along the edge of her tights, just like I was doing—down across the edge of her stomach, from hip to hip and back again. Her stomach quivered beneath my touch and her mouth fell open so she could drag her teeth along my shoulder. She wanted me to know she liked it.

Of course you do, Lily. You told me yourself, you've never been fucked by someone who knew what he was doing.

I slipped my hand beneath the waistband of her tights and then lower, trailing my finger along the outside of her panties. I had her in my hands, so completely open for me. She sighed against me, keeping her focus on my shoulder.

Shy.

She couldn't look me in the eye as I slid my finger past the hem of her panties. She bit down harder on my shoulder, and I held up her weight. She was putty and if I let go, she'd fall to a heap on the floor. I backed us up to the wall, right between my framed photos. I slipped my hand out of her pants and tugged them down, taking in the

125

sight of her naked body. She was tiny, with perky breasts and slim lines, and those hipbones that shouldn't have been visible. She looked so young standing there that I took a step back, thrown for a loop.

I scanned across her tan skin, memorizing the freckle that sat two inches above her left nipple. Now it was my freckle. A secret patch of skin that I hadn't had the time to notice on the yacht.

"Dean?" She spoke with a shaky voice. "I'm on the pill. If that's what you're worried about…"

She thought I didn't want her. She thought I was stepping away for good.

"How old are you Lily." It was part question, part statement.

"Twenty-three."

Ten years difference.

"How many men have you been with?"

She reached out and grabbed my pants, using them to yank me toward her. She was a wolf in sheep's clothing.

"Enough to know how this goes. You're going to take off those pants and push me back against this wall. Maybe you'll hold my hands above my head or maybe you'll grip my chest. I know you want me, Dean."

She slipped her hand beneath the waistband of my pants and gripped me, hard.

"Stop making me wait."

Fuck her.

I had planned on pinning her to the wall, but not any more. She wasn't in control; she might be a feisty young lioness, but I was a lion. I pushed off my pants, gripped her hand, and yanked it off me. Her mouth fell open in shock, but there wasn't time for her to question my actions. I was already lifting her up, forcing her legs around my hips. I had to fight the urge to groan. She felt like heaven and I wasn't even inside her yet.

I walked us up the stairs, toward my bedroom, but it wasn't for romantic reasons. I needed leverage. I needed her on my bed so I could hold my body up over her and angle inside her so deep that her head rolled back and she had to bite her lip to keep from screaming.

The last coherent thought I had that night was when I stood at the end of my bed, staring down at Lily spread across my navy sheets. She was a sea of blonde hair and full, pink lips. I was going to lose myself in her, more than I'd lost myself in anyone before.

She smirked and arched a brow. "Do you need help with that?"

I was holding the condom in my hand, staring at her.

I shook my head.

They say if you aren't sure if a berry is poisonous, you're supposed to touch it first, rub it on your skin, and see if you have a physical reaction. After that, you take a lick and wait a day. Still breathing? Take a small bite. If you're not dead, then the berry is probably safe to eat.

I feared Lily was poisonous. I feared she'd make my heart stop, but instead of testing her touch and tasting her slowly, I slipped into her until her nails dug into my back. I bit down on her lip so hard as she came that I tasted her blood in my mouth.

For all I knew, I had hours to live. For all I knew, Lily would be the death of me.

I smiled at the thought.

What a way to go…

CHAPTER TWENTY-FIVE

LILY

I WOKE UP with a start in a dark room, lying on the softest sheets I'd ever felt in my life. *Am I dead? Is this a cloud?* I inhaled a deep breath and glanced to my right. Dean was lying next to me on his chest. His face was angled toward me and half smashed into his pillow, but he was still the most picturesque thing I'd ever seen. The moonlight illuminated a fading set of teeth marks on his shoulder. *Mine.* I smiled at the memory as I slipped the sheet off my legs and pressed up out of his bed.

A quick glance at his bedside clock announced the time in bright red numbers: 4:30 AM.

I tiptoed across his room, wholeheartedly aware of my nakedness. My thighs ached and there was a light bruise on the left side of my ribcage. Dean had been rough at times, just enough to thrill me, but even then, I'd known I'd be feeling the aftereffects in the morning. I flushed just thinking about it.

I pulled open his door as quietly as possible and didn't bother looking back. I'd see him at the airport in a few hours anyway.

My leggings and tank top were still on the marble floor of the entryway, passing judgment on me as I descended the staircase. I'd had casual sex before, but nothing about last night had been *casual*.

I slipped into my clothes, listening for any sign of Dean. It's not that I didn't want to see him, I just needed five minutes to collect my thoughts. I'd come to his house on a whim, assuming I'd have really good sex and then be on my way. Instead, Dean had reached inside and scattered pieces of me across his house. My sanity sat on his front stoop, my self-control was splattered across his entryway, and my heart was up there on his bed, too tangled in scattered sheets to find.

Walking through the streets of New York at 4:30 AM wasn't on my bucket list, but I didn't have a choice. There were no cabs roaming the streets of the Upper West Side and I was too scared to go down into the subway stations. I'd already walked two miles south before I remembered Uber. Fucking Uber. I requested a ride on the app and a few minutes later a small Romanian woman with a head-wrap pulled up in front of me in a white Buick.

"You Lily?" she asked with a thick accent.

I nodded, slipped into her backseat, and typed in my address.

She peered back and scanned over my outfit. "You always run this early?"

"No."

She veered out into traffic without looking—which was fine since we were the only car on the road—and then glared back at me. "Good. Bad for your knees. Running."

I stared out the window. *You know what else is bad for your knees? Wrapping them around Dean Harper's hips.*

By the time I arrived back at my apartment, I was ready for a full night of sleep. I wanted to crawl onto my futon and burrow myself under the covers so far that I would never wake up again. Unfortunately, when I pushed the door open, I was greeted by a wide-awake and frantic Josephine.

"You idiot! You stupid idiot!" she said, waving a spatula in the air like she was going to hit me with it. Had she even slept? Or had she been awake the whole night stewing because I wouldn't answer her phone calls?

I dropped my purse on the table near the door and shook my head. "You're not allowed to be mad at me for sleeping with Dean."

Her eyes widened. "I'm not mad about that! I'm mad because you just walked home by yourself at 4:30 AM. Dean called me twenty minutes ago demanding to know where you were."

My heart stopped. "He called you? This morning?"

She narrowed her eyes and studied me. "Of course. You left and he had no clue where you went. That was really stupid, Lily."

Knowing he'd woken up, knowing he cared that I was out by myself did a weird thing to my heart. The sick, selfish part of me wanted him to be up, worried about me.

Josephine huffed and turned back toward the kitchen, and finally, I registered the smell of fresh pancakes. *That explains the spatula.*

"It's not like I could go out looking for you," she said, answering my unspoken question. "So I decided to make breakfast for when you got here."

I smirked and walked closer to the kitchen. "I could

have been dead out on the streets, and you'd be here, enjoying your fluffy pancakes."

She glared at me, still pissed. "Pancakes soothe me."

I edged around the counter, dropped my head on her shoulder, and flashed her my best attempt at puppy dog eyes. "Remember when I babysat you that night you got super drunk last month? When you fell into the ditch and couldn't get out?"

She groaned. "Please don't ever remind me of that."

"Well, now we're even, okay?"

She pointed to the plate of warm pancakes sitting beside the stove. "Fine. Eat up and let Dean know that you're home safe."

My stomach clenched at the reminder of Dean. I knew I had to text him; only a true psychopath would let him worry for nothing. I went to retrieve my phone from my purse and found the evidence of his worry: two missed calls and three texts messages.

Dean: Did you leave?

Dean: I just searched my entire house looking for you.

Dean: Call me when you get home.

I skipped the call and instead shot him a quick text.

Lily: Home.

One word. One word that would guard my heart and make it impossible for him to know how affected I was by the last twelve hours.

"Anyway, how was it? Last night?" Jo asked behind me. I swallowed and stared down at my phone.

The pretend answer, the answer I fed to Josephine and kept repeating to myself, was that the night was fun, simple, "nothing serious".

The real answer, the answer that I would never utter aloud, was that it had been life-changing. I'd laid on Dean's bed, staring up at the ceiling with his head between my legs, and I'd begged the universe to freeze. I'd gripped his hand in mine and pleaded for one more second, one more hour, one more night.

But then I'd woken with a start a few hours later, sad to find that the universe didn't pause…not even for me.

CHAPTER TWENTY-SIX

LILY

THE SUITCASE I'D borrowed from Jo had a wheel that rattled nonstop. I would have checked it at the entrance had Dean not explicitly forbidden us from doing so. *"We don't have time to wait for bags when we get to Vegas. Pack light."* I cursed him in my head as the wheel got stuck for the fifth time since entering the airport. I kicked it back into alignment and then locked eyes with the girl standing in front of me in line at the airport Starbucks.

She was wearing Uggs and jean shorts, and rolled her eyes at the audacity of my squeaky wheel. She turned back to her friend and leaned in. "Soo ratchet."

Did she think she was whispering? I could hear every word she said and I desperately wanted to tell her that "ratchet" wasn't a real word—not unless she was working from the Kardashian-Webster Dictionary.

"Oh my god, she's *so* basic," her friend said, angling back to get a good look at me. I tilted my head and smirked. I knew these girls. They were the type to sit behind their iPhones and tweet mean shit out into the world.

When they made it to the front of the line, I listened as they ordered two caramel macchiatos with skim milk and warned the barista behind the counter, "Don't be stingy with the caramel sauce."

He nodded and accepted their cash, all the while probably cursing them to hell alongside me. When it was my turn to order, I got a coffee and then leaned closer. "If I pay you five bucks, will you make their macchiatos with whole milk instead of skim?"

He smirked. "Lady, you don't even have to pay me. I already did it."

I laughed, left five dollars in his tip jar, and felt much better about the world as I walked away, squeaky wheel and all.

When I arrived at our gate—five minutes behind schedule—the rest of the team was already seated with their laptops and iPads on their laps. Hunter and Zoe were on one side of the aisle and Julian and Dean sat across from them. Hunter shot me a narrowed glance when he caught sight of me, but I didn't care. *Narrowed eyes beats flirty comments any day.* Julian was busy on his phone, so I just smiled and rolled past.

When I registered Dean's outfit, I knew I'd made a mistake. I'd slipped on a sundress and Converse before heading to the airport. Dean was wearing a navy suit, shined shoes, and an expression that warned me away.

The only evidence that he was less prepared than normal was the short stubble across his jaw. I liked it.

"Good of you to join us," he said. His deep voice reminded me of what he'd sounded like the night before, when he'd pulled my hair back and whispered dirty thoughts in my ear.

Zoe patted the leather seat beside her and I jumped slightly. "Lily, come sit and tell me if you like these shoes. I've been eyeing them for the last few weeks."

I glanced back at Dean to see if maybe he'd rather I sit by him, but he was focused on his laptop. I'd been in his bed less than twelve hours before and he was already ignoring me. I wheeled my suitcase toward Zoe and sat. The leather was cold on the backs of my thighs and I couldn't concentrate on anything she said. She was talking about shoes and pointing out different color combinations. The entire time, I was acutely aware of Dean. Every time he moved, my gaze flicked over to him. When he took a phone call, I listened with attentive ears. When he tilted his head from side to side, stretching out his neck, I wondered if he was sore from our night.

When we boarded the plane, Zoe slid into the vacant seat beside mine, and Dean and Julian took the seats diagonally across the aisle from us. I couldn't see him without sitting on my heels.

"What are you doing?" she asked.

I flicked my gaze away from the sliver of his head that I could see and sat lower in my seat.

"Nothing," I said, reaching into my purse for...what? *Grab something, you idiot.*

I pulled out my wallet, pretended like I was counting my bills, and then shoved it back inside my purse. The entire time, Zoe stared at me like I was a crazy person. "Got everything you need?"

I laughed nervously. "Good to go."

She arched a brow. "I think you need to relax."

I opened my mouth to reply, but she was already

turning toward the aisle in pursuit of the flight attendant. Too bad for her, the attendant—a pretty brunette with a cute little pair of wings positioned directly beside her cleavage—was already leaning down and flirting with Dean.

"Nah, I'm good. I think I'll go with a water," he said, smiling up at her.

He never smiled at me.

"Are you sure?" She winked. "You are headed to Vegas after all."

He shook his head.

"How about I bring you a water and *something else*?" she insisted. "On me?"

What, like your vagina in a cup? Jesus.

"Yoohoo," Zoe said, waving her hand in the air and cutting off the flight attendant's flirting. She turned toward us and I saw the nametag pinned to her top: Beatrice. "Yes, hi Beatrice. Sorry to interrupt, but I think Dean is good with water, and my friend and I would really love vodka cranberries."

I sank lower in my seat and tried to hide my blush.

"Zoe, behave. This is a work trip," Dean said, condemning her drink choice. I rolled my eyes, though he couldn't see behind the headrest.

"I don't have any meetings today. I can drink *one* vodka cranberry."

"You may not have any meetings, but Lily and I have one as soon as we land."

I jumped out of my chair. "What?"

The last itinerary I'd seen listed events starting the following day.

Dean's gaze sliced up to me. That jaw was set and his piercing brown eyes had no room for love in them when they were so filled with hate.

"I would have told you had you given me the chance."

I swallowed and glanced away. We could have easily been referencing a different topic all together, but with Dean, I could never tell.

"Just email me the new itinerary so we're all on the same page."

"Already did," he said, turning around in his seat and effectively dismissing me. "Check your inbox."

I turned to my phone and pulled up my inbox, curious to see what he'd written.

From: Zoe Davis
To: Lily Black
Subject: FWD: LVRW Itinerary Update

Begin forwarded Message:

From: Dean Harper
To: Zoe Davis
Subject: Itinerary Update

I've attached an updated Itinerary for Lily. Make sure she gets it.

D. Harper

The asshole hadn't even emailed it to me himself.

CHAPTER TWENTY-SEVEN

LILY

LILY WAS POISON, just as I'd feared she would be. I'd woken up in my bed to find her gone, no sign of her anywhere except for the lingering scent of her hair on my pillow. I'd felt like a fool chasing a ghost around my house at 4:30 AM. She could have at least had the decency to leave me a note, but instead she disappeared, ignored my calls, and shot me a one-word text: "Home."

When I first spotted her at the airport, I felt like I'd been punched in the stomach. Lily in a sundress, tan and glowing, was a sight that didn't belong on a business trip. Whereas I felt like shit from my lack of sleep, Lily was radiant. Her blonde hair was twisted up in a bun, revealing the slender slope of her neck and collar bone.

Had she not snuck out of my house in the middle of the night, maybe I would have given her a warmer welcome, but I was pissed. My patience with her was shot and it was only the first day of our Vegas convention.

I worked through the entire plane ride, doing my best to block out her and Zoe's laughter. Eventually, the flight attendant brought me a pair of headphones with a little wink. *She probably wouldn't have left my house at four in the morning*, I thought as I took them from her and blocked out the sound of Lily.

By the time we arrived at the Bellagio, I was exhausted.

"Oh, VIP check-in? Very fancy," Zoe quipped as I lead the group past the front of the lobby. The Bellagio was packed with people waiting to start their Vegas vacation. Sweaty tourists in Hawaiian shirts fidgeted on their feet, anxious and impatient.

"I rented one of their private villas for a few days. It was the only thing available."

Everyone nodded, seemingly impressed. "Unfortunately, it's a three bedroom."

Julian arched a brow. "I could have made arrangements at a different hotel."

Lily's eyes widened. "No. You have to stay with us."

I knew she was nervous. This was her first big work trip and she thought Julian was her only ally. I could have been her ally had she not left at 4 AM.

"Don't be ridiculous," I said to Julian. "You can have your own room. I'll bunk with Hunter and the girls can take the last room."

Zoe coughed. "No can do. I snore. Like really bad."

Lily laughed. "Is there a couch? I'll just sleep on that."

I nodded and spun around before Lily could see my shocked face. Most women I'd dated would have cut my balls off if I'd suggested that they sleep on a couch.

"Do I have time to change before our meeting?" Lily asked, sidling up beside me at the check-in counter. This was supposed to be VIP, but there was no one manning the desk. I pushed the bell two more times and finally slid my gaze to Lily.

"Actually, I won't be needing you at the meeting any more."

Her face fell. "What do you mean?"

"The meeting with Antonio Acosta is tomorrow. That's what I want you to focus on. The meeting today is just with a graphic designer I may hire."

She nibbled on her bottom lip and then her eyes shot up to me with excitement. "I could still go with you. I'd like to see what kind of graphics—"

I cut her off with a sharp shake of my head. "No need."

Finally, a skinny kid in a suit two sizes too big for him pushed open the door from behind reception. He looked flustered and the sweat coating his brow warned me not to berate him for making us wait.

"Hello, I'm sorry. I was helping another guest with a, er, *bathtub situation*."

He faltered at the end of his sentence and Zoe started laughing. Clearly some kinky shit was going down in the rooms of the Bellagio.

The kid's face went beet red and he started typing away on his computer. "What name is the reservation under?"

"Dean Harper."

The entire time he checked us in, I tried to ignore Lily's presence beside me. She seemed hurt that I didn't want her at the meeting any more, but that didn't make sense. She was the one who'd wanted to leave my house before the crack of dawn. She couldn't get away from me fast enough. I stared down at her hands, clasped in front of her dress. She was picking at her nail, focusing all of her attention on that one cuticle. Those hands had been around my neck, gripping onto me for dear life just a few hours earlier.

"Lily," I said hesitantly, unsure of where my sentence would lead.

Her gaze shifted to me and she offered up a fake, flat smile. "Have fun at your meeting. Zoe talked about hitting the pool, so I guess I'll join her."

"Woohoo! Let's go now, Lil. This is dullsville."

Lily turned back to her and laughed. "I guess the guys can take our bags to the villa."

Julian nodded. "Go ahead. I got your stuff."

She thanked him and bent down to retrieve her bikini from her suitcase. It was a little white string thing and suddenly I wasn't sure I wanted her to go to the pool.

"Sir. *Sir?*"

The kid was trying to get my attention so he could explain the hotel policies, but I was watching Lily walk away with Zoe. Fucking Zoe. She was a bad influence.

Julian nudged me in the shoulder. "Can you sign the papers so we can go to our room already? I need to call Jo."

I shook my head and turned back to the reception desk. Once the papers were signed and I had five room keys in hand, Hunter, Julian, and I set off to find the villas. Hunter took the lead with the hotel attendant, helping to ensure none of the bags fell off the cart.

"You want to tell me about last night?" Julian asked, blindsiding me.

I slid my gaze to him. "That was quick."

Julian narrowed his eyes. "News travels. You realize how terribly this could end, right?"

"It won't. Nothing will change."

He chuckled in disbelief. "Those sound like some famous last words if I've ever heard them."

I ignored him and checked my watch. My meeting was set to start in thirty minutes and I still needed to confirm the location. "I'm going to head back to the lobby. Could you make sure Lily's bags get placed in the third bedroom? I'll take the couch."

Julian chuckled. "Wait, what's that? Is Dean Harper actually putting someone else's needs before his own?"

I glared at him. "Wait, what's that? Did you just offer up your bed for me? What a good friend."

He laughed and started walking backward to catch up with Hunter and the hotel attendant. "Sorry man, didn't hear that last part. I'm sure that couch will be really comfy!"

CHAPTER TWENTY-EIGHT

LILY

IF I SAW one more slot machine or frozen daiquiri, I was going to lose it. I'd been in Vegas for twenty-four hours, prepared to work, and instead, I'd lounged by the pool and worked on my tan lines. I should have been involved with the graphic design meeting the day before, but Dean was keeping me out of the loop on purpose. Fortunately, that was about to change.

"What time is your meeting with Antonio Acosta supposed to end?" Zoe asked from the bathroom door.

I paused with my mascara wand a few inches from my face and met her eyes in the mirror. "Probably around five."

She nodded. "Okay cool. I think we'll all get dinner and then the convention is hosting this meet and greet at The Bank later."

"The bank?" I asked, narrowing my eyes.

She laughed. "It's a club inside the casino."

I nodded.

"You'll probably have time to change before that," she said, scanning down my outfit. I was wearing a white button down tucked into a dark red pencil skirt. My nude heels were a sensible height and my makeup was minimal. All in all, I looked like I was running for Congress.

"You don't like my outfit?" I asked.

She narrowed her eyes, pretending to study my prim and proper attire. "I mean, I think you could stand to unbutton that shirt a bit, but if you're going for the Quaker look, that's cool too."

I laughed. I *was* going for the Quaker look. I wanted to look older than twenty-three. I needed Antonio and Dean to take me seriously at the meeting, especially after the way Dean had treated me the day before.

"Lily, are you almost ready?" Dean's voice boomed through the villa. "We need to head out."

Zoe puffed up and tapped her wrist as if she were wearing an imaginary watch. "Mr. Punctual is ready for you!"

I concealed my laugh. "Yes!" I yelled back. "Just two more seconds."

I finished swiping on my mascara and then rubbed lip balm across my lips. Zoe did her best to distract me, but I ignored her reflection in the mirror.

"Don't you have a meeting or something?" I asked as I adjusted my watch.

She grinned. "I had two this morning while you were getting your beauty sleep."

Ah, yes. I *had* gotten beauty sleep—in a bed that should have been Dean's. When Zoe and I had returned to our villa the night before, I'd found my bags inside the third bedroom. Julian insisted Dean wanted me to have it, but

Dean hadn't been around to ask. I'd laid down on the king size bed covered in soft linens and plush pillows, and figured Dean would come yank me out of it if he wanted me on the couch.

He hadn't, and I was eternally grateful.

"Lily!" Dean yelled.

I rolled my eyes and yanked my tote bag over my shoulder. "I'm coming!"

I pushed past Zoe and found Dean standing in the foyer of the villa, staring down at his watch. He'd avoided me for the last twenty-four hours, but we were about to go to a meeting together so he'd have to at least acknowledge my presence.

He was wearing navy pants and a light blue shirt. The top few buttons were undone and his dark brown leather shoes matched his leather belt. The wave in his hair was tamed away from his face and his jaw was clean-shaven again. He looked as debonair as Cary Grant and for a moment I second-guessed my outfit.

He pulled open the door. "C'mon. The meeting is across the hotel."

He was being impatient with me for no reason. We were thirty minutes ahead of schedule and I'd spent the morning going over the list of questions I had for Antonio. I was more than prepared.

"Did you have a productive day yesterday?" I asked as we hit the back entrance of the hotel.

"It wasn't a total waste," he replied as his fingers worked away on his phone.

"Zoe and I ran topless through the hotel yesterday," I said, to see if he was paying attention. "It was really fun."

His brown eyes sliced over to me without a trace of humor. "I hope you spent your time a little more productively than that."

Oh my god. I wanted to strangle him. Where was his sense of humor? Where was his fun side?

"Well, well, look who it is."

I turned toward the voice and found Antonio Acosta standing near the entrance of the ballroom. He was wearing a chef's coat over black pants and flashed us a friendly smile as we approached. He was younger than I'd expected, maybe mid-thirties.

After shaking Dean's hand, he turned his attention toward me and beamed. "Ah, I didn't realize Dean would be bringing a beautiful woman as his date for the meeting."

I smiled and held out my hand. "Lily Black. I'm consulting on the menu for Dean's new restaurant."

His bright, almost amber eyes lit up. "And she's familiar with the arts? Where did you find this one, Dean?"

Dean smiled good-naturedly, but it didn't reach his eyes.

"Come, come. The hotel has partitioned off a small section of this ballroom for us," Antonio said, pressing his hand to the small of my back and ushering us into the room. The expansive ballroom was much too large for what we needed. The ceilings were nearly twenty feet high and long ornate curtains were drawn to keep out the afternoon sun. There was a small round table set up in the corner nearest the door. A row of tea candles lined the center and a white tablecloth draped over the sides. Antonio pulled one of the two chairs out for me and I smiled up at him in thanks.

"The hotel is allowing me to use the kitchen attached to this ballroom. I've spent the morning creating the dishes I had in mind for your restaurant."

I smiled as he picked up my napkin from beside my

plate. He popped it open with a flick of his wrist and then draped it across my lap. I could feel Dean's eyes on us, but he held his tongue until Antonio had excused himself to get the first dish.

"Please don't encourage him."

I retrieved my notes from my tote bag and shook my head. "I'm not."

He grunted and pocketed his phone. Apparently, this meeting was worthy of his undivided attention.

A moment later, Antonio backed out of the swinging door with two small plates in hand. A rich garlic flavor wafted through the room as he stepped closer and set down a plate in front of each of us. My smile fell as I registered the dish.

"I'm starting you two off with a simple dish called gambas al ajillo. It's fresh shrimp sautéed in olive oil infused with garlic. I've also added a touch of Spanish paprika and brandy."

Antonio Acosta was the most sought after Spanish chef in the United States and he was starting us off with *this?* Before Dean's bite reached his mouth, I shook my head.

"I'm sorry, but I have to cut right to it. There's nothing unique in this recipe." I pointed to the plate where four limp shrimp sat in a bath of olive oil.

Dean's gaze met mine and I could see the warning there. He wanted me to proceed with caution, but I couldn't. I'd spent an entire semester on Spanish cuisine, and by the time I'd finished, I knew my tapas. For the ungodly sum of money Antonio was being paid for this tasting, he'd just opened with the tapas equivalent of PB&J. He should have known better.

Antonio swallowed and nodded slowly. "I see. As a chef, I like to honor culinary tradition while striving for measured amounts of uniqueness," he explained deftly. "But let's not dwell on it, let's move on to the next dish."

He reached forward and yanked the plates from the table before Dean could set down his spoon. Clearly, I'd offended him.

Dean arched a brow at me after Antonio had disappeared back into the kitchen. "Next time let me taste the dish before you overstep your bounds and insult the chef."

I narrowed my eyes quizzically at him. He'd brought me there as a consultant, so I was *consulting*.

We sat in silence until Antonio brought out the next dish. It was a slight alteration of another standard tapas dish: patatas bravas. Instead of using Tabasco sauce, he'd swapped in a chipotle mayo for us to dip the potatoes into. The dish was good. Was it worthy of being on our menu? No. Every food critic in New York would pan us.

And that's how the tasting went. Antonio's dishes fell flat every single time. The ingredients were expected. The flavors were standard. There was nothing unique about his presentation and I doubted Antonio had even spent more than five minutes coming up with recipes for our restaurant. Either he was lazy, or he was purposely sabotaging our menu.

I shook my head. "This dish is served in every tapas restaurant in America," I said, pointing at the short ribs in front of me. "Where's the creativity? Where's the effort?"

"Excuse me?" Antonio asked, rearing back as if I'd struck him. For twenty minutes, he'd brought out dishes for us to sample, and for twenty minutes I'd held my tongue as best as possible.

"Lily that's enough," Dean spoke up with a sharp tongue.

I flinched. "Are you serious?"

Dean tossed his napkin onto the table and shook his head. "Let's go. You're excused from the rest of the meeting."

My cheeks flamed as he pushed his chair back and crossed around to escort me from the room. I saw red as I reached down for my bag. He was being taken advantage of and now he was punishing me for standing up for him?

Dean pushed the ballroom door open so hard that it swung back and hit the wall.

"That was completely unprofessional. What were you thinking?" he hissed, reaching up to grip my arm so I couldn't storm off.

"You're delusional. That man is taking advantage of you, and if you don't see that, you're blind."

"He's one of the most influential chefs in America. If his dishes are bad, you eat them and discuss the rest with me after the meeting is over. This is my business, *my* name you're tarnishing by acting like a picky toddler."

I stepped closer. "He just served us glorified french fries. How much did you pay him for that meeting, Dean? Ten thousand dollars? Fifteen?"

"I don't care if he scraped the gunk off his shoe and passed it off as escargot. You have to understand how this world works. Until you do, you can head home. Pack your bags. I don't need you in Vegas any more."

I could feel the flush spread from my cheeks, down across my chest. He could have stabbed me in the heart and it would have hurt less than those eight words. *I don't need you in Vegas any more.*

I'd slept with him less than forty-eight hours earlier and since then he'd ignored me, chastised me, and now he was dismissing me like I was last week's trash.

"Fuck you, Dean," I hissed, shoving my finger into his chest. "Fire me if you think that's what's best, but don't think you can just tuck me away when it's convenient for your ego."

"Don't test me Lily," he said, bending low so that his lips were aligned with mine.

I flashed him a dark, sardonic smile, scraping together my last bit of self-confidence. "Have a great rest of your meeting. I'll see you at the meet and greet later."

"Lily!"

I ignored him and walked away.

CHAPTER TWENTY-NINE

LILY

MY CONFIDENCE BROKE down somewhere in the middle of the Bellagio lobby. I had tears streaking down my cheeks and everyone was subtly getting the hell out of my way, pulling their children away from me like I was deranged. *I'm not going to attack your kid just because I'm crying. Jeez.*

I walked past the pool, remembering how naive I'd been the day before. I'd lounged on those chairs and assured myself that Dean had brought me to Vegas because he respected me and valued my opinion, no matter how strong it might be. Perhaps I'd overstepped my bounds in that meeting, but that was no reason to send me home. He'd just treated me like scum and he thought I was going to go hide away and lick my wounds? If he thought that was a possibility, then he really didn't know me at all.

I pushed through the door to our private villa and thanked all the gods of awkward moments that it was empty. I hated having to be there. If I could have, I would have grabbed my bags and found my own room, but the hotel was completely booked, and let's face it, I couldn't have afforded my own room anyway. The living room, with the sectional Dean had slept on the night before, was quiet and empty. The courtyard with its fruit trees and ivy vines remained untouched.

I bypassed the mini bar, the giant kitchen, and the gym. *Who needs a gym? I'm not working out on a work trip. The same rules of vacation apply.* I shut myself in my room and sneered at the opulent decor. I'd appreciated it the day before, but now it just made me want to barf. This was *Dean's* villa, and I hated it.

I reached for the phone beside my bed and dialed Jo's number, praying she'd answer.

"Are you calling to gossip? What happened to 'blah blah blah stays in Vegas'?" she asked as soon as the call connected.

I smiled, though it felt wrong. "How'd you know it was me?"

"Lucky guess. What are you doing? Aren't you busy? Julian said he was going to explore the casino before the meet and greet later."

"I just got kicked out of a meeting, so it looks like I have the rest of the afternoon to myself."

"What do you mean? Who booted you?"

"Dean."

"Are you serious?"

I nodded, though she couldn't see me. "He's not like Julian. I don't even know how they can be friends. They're so different."

"I'm sorry, Lily."

"I'm tempted to book an earlier flight and come home. I don't care what it costs me."

"What? Are you serious? You're going to throw in the towel and come home? Who are you and what have you done with Lily Black?"

"Ha ha."

"I think you should stay and give Dean a taste of his own medicine. You've never let someone get away with treating you like that. Do you remember in the third grade when you cut off Betsy Higgins' pigtail because she stole your Lisa Frank folder?"

I laughed.

"Seriously. Take that little black dress out of your suitcase, add a little smoky eye, and get your ass down to that club."

I stared down at Josephine's black lace dress sitting on the top of my luggage. When I'd tried it on at home, the material on the bodice had curved perfectly around my breasts and sloped up to a thin halter that buttoned behind my neck. I knew if I put it on, I'd gain back a sliver of the confidence Dean had stolen earlier that day.

"How'd you know I have that dress?"

"Because I have an empty hanger in my closet where it should be. That thing had better not stay in Vegas."

Damn, she was good.

"I promise I won't get anything on it," I said, stepping closer and running my fingers over the lace.

"Don't worry about that. Send me a picture of you after you get ready. I'll be living vicariously through you."

I stared up at myself in the mirror. My hair was flat and my mascara was smeared beneath my eyes. I'd need a major overhaul if I intended on meeting the group at the club downstairs in a few hours.

"I'll make you proud," I said, pulling the dress out of the suitcase and then reaching for a pair of black strappy heels that I'd nabbed as well. "PS, I also have your black Manolos. Okayloveyoubye."

I crammed all the words together and hung up before she could berate me for stealing her shoes as well. She immediately shot me a text.

Josephine: Don't let Dean's tears ruin those shoes.

I didn't want Dean to weep; I wanted him to realize how wrong he was. He didn't take me seriously as a friend or as a coworker. He underestimated me just like everyone else, and that night, I planned on proving him wrong.

I reached for the hotel phone, dialed the front desk, and asked to be connected to the salon.

After I'd scheduled a hair and makeup appointment, I hung up, grabbed everything I needed for the evening, and headed for the salon. I was standing in the central elevator bank, waiting for a lift when a family joined me. I glanced over to see a little girl staring up at me, confused by the mascara on my cheeks. I'd forgotten to wash it off before leaving my room.

"Mommy, can I get my face painted like a monster too?" the little girl whispered loudly.

I smiled and turned back to the illuminated numbers above the elevator.

Not a monster. *A phoenix.*

CHAPTER THIRTY

DEAN

"ARE YOU AN idiot?" Zoe asked.

"You asked her to *go home?*" Julian was in complete disbelief.

My explanations fell on deaf ears: she'd been disrespectful, she'd jeopardized a relationship that had taken me years to cultivate, and she was a constant threat to my self-control. I didn't tell them the last reason, of course. They'd have a field day with that knowledge, especially because it was the only reason that really mattered. She'd been out of line in the meeting with Antonio, but hardly terrible enough to send home. No, I wanted her gone because having her in Vegas was a constant reminder of my struggle. I could look, but not touch. I could berate her for screwing up a meeting, but I couldn't kiss her. I'd slept on the couch, ten feet from her, and I'd lain awake the entire night, listening and praying I'd hear a sound coming from her room, some kind of invitation. Nothing had come and I was tired as shit.

She needed to go. It was the only way I could focus for the second half of the week.

Still, a part of me hoped she'd meant what she'd said as she'd walked away earlier.

I'll see you at the meet and greet later.

● ● ●

The Bank was filled to the brim with industry people. I recognized half of them from years past, and the other half I'd read about in the food sections of newspapers and magazines.

The celebrity chefs already had crowds around them and I steered clear, opting for a table across the room. Hunter, Zoe, and Julian followed me in, taking in the scene in silence. I ordered bottle service and threw Zoe a pleading look. She shrugged and stared down at her phone. *Good enough.* I couldn't stand another hour of her anger.

Our waiter returned with bottles of Hendrick's Gin and Deep Eddy Vodka. I watched him set out ice, glasses, and a slew of mixers. Once he was gone, I motioned for them to make their drinks first and turned to scan the room.

I couldn't admit to myself that I was looking for Lily until I found her. Her long blonde hair was curled and slipping down across her back. Her black dress was tight and short. I scanned down her tan legs and then lingered on her, too aware of the kick drum in my chest.

She laughed and reached out to touch the arm of the guy across from her. It was nothing more than a harmless gesture, but the guy's smile almost split his face in two. I couldn't blame him; I knew what that touch felt like.

Hunter, Julian, and Zoe were talking behind me, carrying on an entire conversation that I ignored. Someone tapped my shoulder, but I was too interested in Lily, too aware of her movements in that black dress. She turned in my direction and her eyes found me. I didn't glance away. It was a challenge, just like always. One slender brow arched in acknowledgement and then she excused herself from the group. Their faces fell and the man she'd touched reached out after her, like he wasn't ready to let her go yet.

Too bad, asshole.

You never even had her.

I watched her walk toward the table like a mirage. If I blinked, if I turned away, she'd disappear.

"Lily!" Zoe yelled, jumping up to greet her.

Lily smiled, but her focus was still on me.

She looked different, like for once she wasn't shying away from her absolute beauty. She was making a show of it, as if she knew exactly the kind of power she wielded.

Her red-stained lips curled into a smirk and she pressed a piece of paper to my chest. I reached for it, gripping her hand along with the slip of paper.

She shook her head and pulled her hand away.

This was a game and the rules were clear: she wasn't mine for the night. I didn't deserve her.

"That sheet of paper has the names and emails of three prominent food bloggers who would like to be invited to our grand opening."

I smiled.

"Jessica Kepner writes a weekly column for the Times. She's a tapas fanatic and wants to do an in-depth interview with you and the team. Her info is on the back. She's expecting you to call her next week."

I thought I might have fallen in love with Lily in that

moment.

She leaned closer so that her lips were a few inches from my face. I focused there as she bit out the last few words. "I might not know as much about this world as you do, but I deserve your best semblance of respect. You don't get to send me home because I didn't kiss that chef's ass. This is my job, and it's time for you to realize that I'm good at it."

She walked away before I could pick my jaw up off the floor. She wasn't going to let me win that easily. Hell, she probably wasn't going to let me win at all. I stood and smiled.

Game on.

• • •

I found Lily by the bar, waiting on a drink.

"Can we talk for a second?" I whispered against her ear. "Alone?"

She ignored me, bending forward to try to get the bartender's attention. Fortunately for me, he had a hundred other customers vying for a drink. I reached out and gripped her arm. Her skin was so soft beneath my fingers, I wanted to trace the curve of her arm, up to her neck and beyond.

She flinched and tried to pull her arm back. "Let go of me, Dean."

"Come talk to me."

She tilted her head and narrowed her smoky eyes up at me. "You know, I think I'd rather stay here. Maybe another time."

She twisted around, trying to walk away, but I still had

a grip on her arm. She winced and I knew I was hurting her, but I couldn't let go. My fingers were wrapped around her arm and if I let her go, she'd slip back into the dim lights of the club, free to do whatever she wanted.

"Lily, you good?"

The guy from earlier—the one who'd hated to see her walk away—was back and about to find my last nerve. His too-tight Izod shirt was tucked into his jeans and the bright salmon color confirmed the fact that he wouldn't know what to do with a woman like Lily if he were ever lucky enough to have her.

"Who's this? Is he hitting on you?"

She laughed and the hollow sound sliced through me.

"No. This is my *boss*."

Her tone was icy and distant. When she turned back to stare at me, I knew I'd lost whatever grip I'd once had on her. My fingers slid from her arm and I stared down at the red imprint I'd caused. It faded almost instantly, her tan overwhelming the redness as she let the guy lead her toward a dark corner of the club. I stood immobile, letting the crowd press into me, jostling and yelling out drink orders I couldn't hear.

CHAPTER THIRTY-ONE

LILY

IT WAS PAINFUL to walk away from Dean. I'd thought it would feel good to take Jo's advice and give him a taste of his own medicine, but it left me on edge. What if that was it? I'd wanted to push a little, but what if I'd pushed him away for good? Was I prepared to see him with another woman? Prepared to never share another night with him?

I grabbed a linen paper towel from the club's bathroom sink and wiped my hands, steering my gaze clear of the mirror. I knew if I looked there it'd be harder to ignore my true desire. The makeup, the dress? It was all for him. I'd told myself it was for the job, that I needed to look my best for the meet and greet, but mostly I'd just wanted Dean to eat his words. I wanted him to see me for the asset that I was and beg for one more night with me.

I shook my head free of those thoughts and pushed through the bathroom door. I could smell Hunter's cologne before I saw him. It was a heavy, spiced scent that felt the same as secondhand smoke when it hit my nostrils.

"There you are, Lily," he mumbled, practically licking his lips.

I sneered. He was one of the few people that made my hair stand on end whenever he was near, and I took it as a sign to stay away from him.

"What do you need, Hunter?"

He stepped forward and the top half of his drink slipped out over the edge. That's when I picked up on his heavy eyelids and half-untucked shirt—the man was three sheets to the wind.

"Lily. Lily. Lily. You're so beautiful. It's so painful to work with you every day."

I swallowed and stepped to the side, toward the end of the hallway. The club was packed, but the small alcove with the bathrooms was annoyingly empty. I didn't think Hunter had it in him to attack, but even so, I wanted to get away from him and his waterlogged words as soon as possible.

"Thanks Hunter," I said with a flat tone. "I'm going to head back out there now."

He frowned and reached into his shirt pocket.

"Wait. Wait. Lily, here. Take this."

He shoved a piece of paper into my hand before I could flinch back.

"It's the room I rented for us. Nobody has to know. Come find me later, baby," he said, trying his best to smirk. At best, it looked like some sort of grimace. At worst, it looked like his lips were falling off.

I shook my head and glanced down at the piece of scrap paper in my hand. On one side of it, there was a logo for Ivy & Wine—a restaurant name I didn't recognize—but when I turned it over, I saw the numbers he'd scrawled. It looked like two 8s and a 4. *Or it maybe a 6...oh, Hunter.*

I tossed the paper into the trash and set off to find Nick. Or was it Rick? *Shit.* He was a food critic from San Francisco and I'd been putting up with his terrible breath for the last two hours in the hopes that he would feature one of Dean's restaurants on his website.

I searched through the club to no avail. Nick-Rick was gone and I needed another drink if I was going to get through the rest of the meet and greet. I'd already handed Dean more than enough names, but I wanted to go above and beyond anything he could imagine. I needed him to know how valuable I was.

The lights in the club changed colors every few seconds, flickering in and out in a rainbow effect. Blue, green, yellow, red. Each moment that passed painted my skin a different hue.

What was Dean doing?

Who was he talking to?

I wedged against the bar and was waiting for the bartender's attention when I felt his hand on my hip. Not Nick-Rick. *Dean.*

His hand gripped my waist, branding me through my dress. I glanced down and his hand skimmed an inch lower. I hated how happy I was that he'd come back. He wasn't done. I could push and push and push, and he would just pull and pull and pull me back.

"You've proved your point," he whispered in my ear.

"Excuse me?" I asked, barely getting the words out without a stutter.

"You're punishing me," he said, his hand biting into my hip. "Enough."

The bartender slapped his towel down onto the bar and met my eye.

"You gonna order or what?" he asked.

"She'll have a lime juice margarita."

"Wrong. I want a dirty martini."

The bartender shook his head, annoyed with the two of us. He bent to retrieve a glass and I was left alone with Dean once again.

"Let go of me," I huffed over my shoulder. "Nick will be back soon."

"Fuck Nick."

I inhaled a sharp breath, registering his anger. He was a nine on the Richter scale and I knew if I pushed him any further, my world would shake because of it.

"You and I are nothing, Dean. We had sex—"

"Mind-blowing sex," he corrected.

I swallowed and chanced a quick glance over my shoulder. He was right there. That jaw, those lips, the scent of his body wash—I wanted it all.

"But as you've clearly shown, we've moved on," I continued.

He took a step closer, pinning me to the bar with his hips. I could feel him against me as he pressed one foot between my legs.

"I'm not done yet," he said.

"Well I am."

The bartender set down my drink. "Here ya go. Do you have a tab?"

Dean threw a few bills down on the bar and reached for the drink. I twisted around and watched as he swallowed down *my* alcohol. He handed the glass over and met my gaze as I brought the drink to my lips. I tasted him on the glass; the martini was nothing compared to him.

He jutted his chin up. "Prove it."

"Prove what?" I asked.

"If it was just sex, then let me take you back to the villa. No harm in round two, right?"

I took another sip of the drink and his fingers skimmed beneath the hem of my dress. He bent low, bringing his mouth parallel to mine.

"Answer me," he demanded as his brown eyes searched my face, landing on my lips with a plea.

He wanted to test me? He thought he could handle round two?

Fine.

I reached down, gripped his hand on my thigh, and yanked it away. Hard.

"Let's go," I said, dropping my forgotten drink back on the bar. I didn't want it any more. Dean had ruined it, just like he'd ruined me.

He mirrored my steps, keeping control of my body. I may have been leading us out of the bar, but it was clear that I was the puppet on his strings. He reached forward and pushed the door open, skimming a kiss along my neck as he stood back to his full height. The goose bumps that bloomed beneath his kiss betrayed my attraction to him. I straightened my shoulders as the doors opened and I took a step out, righting the mission in my head.

Once again, he was trying to wrest the steering wheel out of my hands. I had to do something. I had to get the upper hand.

CHAPTER THIRTY-TWO

DEAN

OUR VILLA WAS tucked into a quiet corner of the property. To access it, we had to take a private path that snaked past the pools and the ballrooms. I held Lily's hand as I led her down the path, and I could feel her body humming like a live wire. When we were nearly at the entrance to our villa, I paused and turned toward her.

"I was harsh earlier. After the meeting—"

She didn't let me finish my apology. She took two steps to close the gap between us and threw her body against mine. I wasn't expecting her assault and my body fell back against the wall before I could stop it. I caught her waist, steadying the two of us before we toppled over. She gripped my face and kissed me like her life depended on it.

"Christ," I hissed as she bit down on my bottom lip. I gripped her arms and tried to pull back, but she didn't let me. She wanted to draw blood.

I growled and pivoted, pushing her back against the

wall. I wedged her against the concrete and wiped the blood from my lip. "You want to play rough, Lily?"

Her eyes looked wicked in the moonlight. Bright and feral and angry.

"I hate you," she said through clenched teeth.

I smiled sardonically. "You bring out the worst in me, you know that? I'm only an asshole around you."

Before she could answer, I gripped her chin and kissed her. My tongue slipped into her mouth and she didn't fight me. Her body was fighting me, her words were fighting me, but that mouth? She was so receptive that for a moment I thought we'd have sex right there against the wall of the private path. That is, until she nearly kneed me in the balls.

"Fuck, Lily," I gasped, narrowly blocking her attack.

She narrowed her eyes and yanked out of my hold. Her keycard was out and she was pushing through the door to the villa before I could catch up to her. The lights were off and the curtains were drawn. For a moment, I didn't want to step in after her. Nothing good would come from us fighting when we were both heated, but she held the door open. Her body was silhouetted by the lights on the path. Her body was an invitation. That neck, the slender dip of her waist, her long legs propped against the door.

"I thought you said there was no harm in round two?" she asked from the doorway.

She was like a villain, leaving a trail of blood and hints meant to lure me into a trap. A man with a mind for self-preservation would have turned and run. Instead, I pushed through the door and locked it behind me. She reached for the light switch and I caught her hand, holding it steady. The darkness fit us. This thing between us was meant for the shadows.

"You told me to go home," she said, stepping forward

and pressing her body against mine.

"It's easier when you aren't around," I whispered, cupping the back of her neck.

"Why? Because you've never been with a woman like me?"

I smiled, but she couldn't see it in the darkness. "I've never *wanted* a woman like you."

"Why's that?"

I kissed her cheek. "I want a woman that makes me feel important. I want someone that appreciates what I do."

"Nobody can make you feel important, Dean. That's why you'll never be satisfied. You want me to tell you how successful you are? You want me to compliment you?"

I couldn't find the words to respond.

"Oh, Dean, *what strong arms you have*."

I smiled.

"Good?" she asked.

"Terrible," I said, taking her ear lobe between my teeth.

"You'd hate a woman like that," she said, slipping her hand beneath the waistband of my pants.

I reached for the zipper of her dress and I slowly pulled it down, splitting the lace apart to expose her soft skin. I dipped my hand beneath the fabric and pushed the zipper lower, following the curve of her spine. I kept pulling her dress down and she kept slipping her hand lower. What a maddening game.

"This is the only thing we're good at," she said, stroking me.

I couldn't disagree.

If I didn't want to kill her, I wanted to possess her. I wanted to seduce her to the brink of madness so that for thirty minutes she could do nothing but moan in my arms, too lost in the moment to hate me.

"Take me to my room," she begged.

I pushed her dress to the floor and kicked it aside. She gripped my tie in her hand and tugged me forward. We were lost in the darkness, tripping over end tables and couches and lamps. We fell into her room and closed the door behind us. The room was just as dark as the rest of the villa, but we found the bed and fell onto it. Her limbs tangled with mine, but I pushed her higher, up against the pillows. She was soft everywhere, but the skin between her thighs was pure velvet. I stripped her down to nothing and she pulled the tie from my neck, nearly choking me before finally getting it off. I think she enjoyed it, that line between hurting someone and loving them. I think that's how she felt about me.

"Lay back," I told her, pushing my hand to her stomach and keeping her flush with the bed.

"I still don't forgive you for what you did earlier."

I smirked and bent low, dragging my tongue up the inside of her left knee. "Maybe you'll find forgiveness after I'm done with you."

She arched her back, pushing up against my hand.

"Never."

CHAPTER THIRTY-THREE

DEAN

LILY STOOD IN the doorway after her shower. She was naked and using one of the oversized hotel towels to dry her legs. I sat on the bed watching her, momentarily sated. We hadn't said anything for what seemed like hours, but I knew the truce wouldn't last long.

"You told me to prove it, and I did."

I frowned, trying to place her words.

"Us," she said, wrapping the towel around her chest. "It's just sex." She smirked. "Dark smoke, but no fire."

She turned and closed the bathroom door without another word. She'd thrown her knife and it had met its mark; the only thing I could do was leave before she threw another.

I was exhausted, especially after the last few hours, but I couldn't find a comfortable spot on the sectional. I angled my body one way, then another, then stood and tried a different direction. The couch felt lumpy in places it hadn't the night before. I stared up at the villa's ceiling and tried to ignore the dull ache in my gut.

My parents' words rang back through my mind.

"You think that fast life will sustain you for long?"

"Aren't you lonely?"

Their questions had always been easy to deflect. I'd moved to New York to become a one-man empire and I'd had no intentions of stopping any time soon. I'd been happy with that life.

One day, I was content, and the next, I was lying on a couch in Vegas with lumps of indecision disrupting my sleep.

I didn't want this.

I didn't want change.

I didn't want to lay awake with a hollow gut and the taste of regret in my mouth. I couldn't build a one-man empire if I lost focus. I'd pushed away every distraction that had come my way in the last two years, yet somehow Lily had seeped through the cracks, like a poison. I just had to find the antidote.

CHAPTER THIRTY-FOUR

LILY

SOMETHING ABOUT DEAN kept me coming back for more. It had been wrong to sleep with him the first time and just plain idiotic to agree to round two. Dean had stripped me to the bone on that hotel bed and then he'd left me high and dry. Well technically he'd left after I'd all but pushed him out, but that was the way we were. He pushed, I pushed back. He didn't want an insipid Barbie. He wanted a challenge, but he kept denying it, so things between us would never change. It was a vicious cycle. I needed an intervention. I needed to cut Dean out of my personal life. Cold turkey.

"Does sitting at a coffee shop across from a cycling studio count as exercise?" Josephine asked as she sat down with her latte.

I blinked away my thoughts and nodded. "The calories transfer. Like osmosis."

She smirked. "So then we should split that banana nut muffin?"

I didn't even turn to inspect the case of pastries behind me. I had no appetite. "I'm good. You go ahead."

She frowned. "I'm sorry, what? The last time you turned down a baked good was because you thought gluten was poisonous."

"That BuzzFeed article made it sound like it was rat poison!" I contested.

She shook her head and took a sip of her latte. I'd arrived at the coffee shop earlier than her, hoping to sample a few of the pastries for my blog. Instead, I'd sat at a table by myself, sipping on my coffee and people-watching through the front windows.

"You've been back from Vegas for a week and you've uttered like four words since then."

I furrowed my brows. "Not true."

"Asking Siri to play James Blunt doesn't count."

I wasn't sure she was right, but I didn't have the energy to fight with her.

"I'm going to set you up with this guy I work with at Vogue."

I scrunched my nose. "I'm not really into male models."

"No, he works in the graphics department. He has a beard and glasses, and sometimes from the right angle, he looks like Bradley Cooper."

I hummed. "The Hangover Bradley Cooper or Silver Linings Playbook Bradley Cooper?"

She seemed confused by my question. "Is there a difference?"

"Big time."

She rolled the question around in her mind and then nodded. "I'd say Silver Linings Playbook Bradley."

"So he's cute but a little psycho?"

"Oh my god, forget it."

I shrugged. *Fine with me.*

She gave me a few minutes, enough time to start people-watching out the window again before she decided to drop her next bomb on me. "Julian says Dean has been hard to work with lately."

My stomach clenched at the mention of his name.

"Worse than usual," she added.

I took a sip of my coffee and purposely stared out at the street above Jo's shoulder.

"You wouldn't know anything about that, would you?"

Fuck her prying.

I forced my gaze to her. "Jo, you and Julian are awesome. You both love each other and you never fight and you're the cutest thing since sliced bread."

"I don't think that's how the saying go—"

"I would love a relationship like you guys have, but unfortunately Dean and I will never be like that."

"Why?"

I laughed. *Where to begin?*

"To start, I don't think he and I have ever had a conversation without one of us yelling. He is rude and opinionated and a workaholic. He has the ego of Kayne West and I hate him."

She ticked off the reasons on her fingers as I spoke. "That's only six things! Pfft, you could totally work through that."

I shook my head. "Add on the fact that he has yet to call or text me since we got back from Vegas."

She frowned. "Have you tried to reach out to him?"

I shot her a 'you're insane' glare.

She held up her hands in surrender. "Maybe you're right. You two are so freaking stubborn."

We were stubborn and I should have hated it, but I

didn't. I *loved* it. I craved a relationship with him. I could hardly wrap my head around what it would be like. Would Dean wake up and make us breakfast in the mornings? Would I pour him coffee? Never. He'd complain that I did it wrong and I'd probably end up pouring it out on his smug face. God, we'd end up pushing each other to the brink of insanity.

I knew that wasn't healthy. I knew that a relationship shouldn't be about two people trying to win the upper hand. Someone had to give. *Right?*

"What's Vogue guy's name?" I asked gently.

Jo peered at me from the top of her latte mug. "Carson."

Carson. *That's not a bad name.*

"Tell Carson I'm free next week if he wants to get like chicken nuggets or something."

Her brows perked up. "Are you serious?"

I downed the rest of my coffee before answering. "I don't kid about chicken nuggets."

She grabbed my shoulders. "Not about the nuggets, you weirdo. I'm asking about the date!"

"Sure. Why not? After all, I am single."

CHAPTER THIRTY-FIVE

DEAN

AFTER VEGAS, I went two weeks before scheduling another team meeting. I focused on my other restaurants and worked in the back office of Provisions, telling myself it was necessary. I sent out work for Hunter, Zoe, and Lily in formal group emails

From: Dean Harper
To: Lily Black, Julian Lefray, Zoe Davis, Hunter Smith
Subject: LVRW

Last week went well. I'm going to take the next few days to play catch-up with Provisions and Merchant. Zoe, I need you as floor manager for the next few nights—

Provisions went to shit while we were gone. Hunter, get in touch with Mark and have him start showing you listings for potential properties. We need to get the ball rolling. I want a list of properties by the end of the week.

D. Harper

From: Lily Black
To: Dean Harper
Subject: Re: LVRW

Just read your last email and you didn't mention me. What would you like me to be working on? Menu? Drinks? Name? Branding?

-Lily

From: Dean Harper
To: Lily Black
Subject: Re: Re: LVRW

Start putting together a list of bloggers we need to invite to the grand opening.

D. Harper

From: Lily Black
To: Dean Harper
Subject: Re: Re: Re: LVRW

Don't you think that's a little premature? We haven't even picked a location yet...

-Lily

From: Dean Harper
To: Lily Black
Subject: Re: Re: Re: Re: LVRW

See last email.

D. Harper

From: Lily Black
To: Dean Harper
Subject: Re: Re: Re: Re: Re: LVRW

Fine, I'll work on the list.

-Lily

● ● ●

DEAN

I tricked myself into thinking that email communication with Lily was harmless, even though every time her name hit my inbox, I felt a familiar rush of adrenaline. Then, two weeks after returning to New York, Antonio Acosta sent me an email and I reluctantly scheduled a team meeting. I'd have to face her whether I wanted to or not.

As I rounded the corner into the employees-only hallway, I could hear the team chatting in the back office and my grip tightened around the papers in my hand at the sound of Lily's voice.

"I feel like I haven't seen you in forever," she said.

"I know. Anything new with you?" Zoe asked.

I rounded the corner of my office and stared at the back of Lily's blonde hair. "Oh god, Jo set me up on a blind date for later this week. I need some advice—"

I stepped into the office and closed the door with a loud slam. Listening to Lily discuss a blind date was on par with getting a root canal. She twisted around to stare daggers at me, but I pretended not to notice. I went around the group and handed each of them a printout of the email I'd received from Antonio the night before. Once everyone had a copy, I took a seat on the edge of my desk and watched them read through it.

Julian finished first, his brows arched to his hairline.

"Wow. I wasn't expecting this," he said.

I nodded and purposely focused anywhere but Lily. I wasn't good about acknowledging the error of my ways, and if I knew her as well as I thought I did, she wasn't going to let the email slide without gloating.

"I'm sorry, maybe I'm confused," she said, staring up at me. "Could you explain what this email means? Just in case I'm reading it wrong?"

Zoe laughed.

She wasn't reading it wrong. She wanted to hear me explain it out loud because she was infuriating.

I crossed my arms and finally let myself look at her. Her full lips were twisted into a smirk and the glint in her eye proved she knew what she was doing. She was wearing a sleeveless blue dress that left her long legs on display. Her hair was pulled over her right shoulder so that I could admire the curve of her neck. She tapped her finger against the email impatiently. She was demanding and breathtaking.

I cleared my throat. "Antonio Acosta sent us a revised list of dishes for our menu. He apologized for his lack of preparedness in Vegas. I don't think he gave a valid excuse as to why his original suggestions were shit. Regardless, the new dishes look great and we will definitely be flying him out soon for another tasting."

Her smirk widened. "Just so we're clear, Antonio sent us revised dishes for no reason whatsoever? Out of the kindness of his own heart?"

I gripped the edge of the desk and I shook my head. "You want me to commend your behavior in that meeting, Lily, but I won't do it. You were rude and disrespectful. On any other day, a chef as hotheaded as Antonio would have smeared us in the press. We're lucky he was feeling generous."

She huffed out a breath of air and crossed her arms.

"Have we decided on the name yet?" Julian asked, changing the subject before Lily and I dominated the rest of the meeting with an argument.

"I'm still working on it. I've got a few in mind though."

"I've been coordinating with the graphic designer you hired in Vegas," Zoe said, directing the meeting toward her work. "Obviously, we can't do much without a name, but we've begun to work on basic branding. You've told us what aesthetic you'd like for the restaurant, so once we have the name we can home in on what logo would work best."

"Have you forwarded me that progress?" I asked.

She nodded. "Everyone should have it in their inbox."

"Good." I turned to Hunter and his eyes widened. "How is the search going for the restaurant space?"

He swallowed and pulled at the collar of his shirt, trying to loosen its hold around his neck. "Um. Yeah. I've been looking, but there's not much out there. Whole lotta rough, not many diamonds."

I narrowed my eyes. That's not what I wanted to hear. "I'm not looking for anything polished, just something we can work with. You're telling me there are no available leases in Manhattan?"

Was that his attempt at a bad joke?

His cheeks flamed. "It's just a tough market right now and I think…it's just…"

He was rambling and it made no sense. Hunter had helped me find the spaces for my last four restaurants and he'd never once had a problem.

"I'll help," Lily offered gently. "I can search around online when I get home."

Hunter shot her a sharp glare. He clearly didn't want her help, but tough shit. He needed it.

"That'd be great. Thanks."

She smiled and the impact of it knocked me off my equilibrium.

"Actually, Lily could you stay after the meeting for a second?"

Her smile faltered. "Oh, uh…sure. Okay."

She was as surprised by my question as I was. The plan was to have a group meeting and then send everyone on their way, together. I should've realized I'd cave as soon as I saw her. Two weeks apart meant that she was more tempting than ever. The desire that should have faded was too sharp to ignore. I had nothing business related to discuss with her; I just wasn't ready for her to walk away yet.

CHAPTER THIRTY-SIX

LILY

ZOE WAS THE last to leave Dean's office. She turned back and shot me a knowing grin just as I shut the door on her. Dean stood behind his desk, peeling off his suit jacket. His corded arm muscles flexed as he tossed it onto the back of his chair.

When his attention was focused on me, I wet my bottom lip and tried to smile. It felt weak.

"I asked you to stay so that we could have a moment alone to talk about the situation between us."

He was putting our relationship into business terms. Dean's opening move was always to treat the issue like it was just another danger to his bottom line, but I knew better. I could see the way his breathing had shifted when I'd turned to him. We were alone in his office. I was a few feet away and he was already daydreaming of the ways he could take me across his desk.

I stepped forward. "I'm completely capable of being

professional around you."

My words said one thing and my tone hinted at the opposite.

His mouth twitched and he bent his head to hide the smirk he didn't want me to see. "I agree. Sleeping with each other doesn't have to interfere with our business relationship."

"Exactly."

"Did I hear that you have a blind date this week?" he asked, arching a brow at me.

"Uh huh. I'm sure you'll keep yourself busy as well." I stepped closer and kicked one shoe off and then the other.

He loosened his tie. "Very busy."

"When's your next meeting?" I asked as I hit the edge of his desk.

He unbuttoned his belt. "I have to be across town in an hour."

I nodded.

"You?"

I smirked. "I'm free all afternoon. I just have to do that property search."

He nodded, then his brown eyes met mine, and in less than a second, the spark between us was ablaze. I dropped my purse on the floor and crawled over his desk. A ballpoint pen fell off and rolled across the floor as his hands gripped my waist and he pulled me all the way over.

It'd been two weeks since his hands had been on me. Fourteen days to go insane. A clean cut with Dean was never truly an option. I knew it had to be messy. I wanted Dean to kiss me like he was kissing me at that very moment. I wanted his hands searing through my skin. His tongue slipped into my mouth and his finger slipped into my panties. I gripped his hair and spread my legs on the edge of his desk. He stood between them, yanking my dress up over my thighs like the material offended him.

"I'll never get enough," he threatened, as I unzipped his pants. I shook with adrenaline as he pushed his pants and boxer briefs down and kicked them aside.

He had me there on the edge of his desk, completely under his thumb.

"You love this as much as I do," he said, skimming his hands up my thighs.

He smiled with such satisfaction as he slipped into me. I dragged my nails down the back of his neck, trying to throw back some of the feeling onto him. I didn't want it. I hadn't asked to have my heart split in two.

He was wrong; I didn't love it as much as him.

I loved it *more*.

CHAPTER THIRTY-SEVEN

LILY

Lily: I'm headed to my blind date right now…

Dean: Where are you meeting him? Don't let him lure you back to his apartment. Jo probably picked a creeper.

I smiled and shoved to the side of the subway car so that people had room to exit. Every stop we passed, the car emptied out a little more, finally leaving some vacant seats. I nabbed one and turned back to my phone.

Lily: We're just going to eat somewhere uptown. I'm meeting him at a park first.

Dean: Romantic.

Lily: Are you seeing someone tonight?

Dean: Not sure yet.

Lily: Don't have sex with her.

Dean: Lily...

Lily: Fine. Whatever. Sleep with whoever you want. Just don't spoil your appetite.

Dean: I'm not the one going on a date right now.

He had a point, but I was going for a very, *very* noble reason: I'd been too busy daydreaming about having sex with Dean and then actually having sex with Dean to remember to cancel on Carson. *See? I'm sure this sort of thing happens to the Dalai Lama ALL the time.*

Whatever. Jo said I couldn't stand him up and I couldn't cancel last minute because that was almost as bad as standing him up. Instead, we agreed that I'd go on one date, and give him a chance. She said I needed to test the water with other guys. Maybe I was into Dean because I was lonely in a new city and there weren't any other guys in my life. I knew better, but she was annoying and I kind of owed her at least one date with a random guy after subjecting her to two weeks of Love Actually on repeat. (*Yes, you actually CAN overdose on Hugh Grant.*)

Dean: Y'know this guy could probably do better. Does he know how stubborn you are?

Lily: I'm sure he'll fall in love at first sight and we'll run away together.

Dean: Hunter will be so disappointed...

I typed back "More than you?" but my finger hovered over the send button. I knew I couldn't actually send it. Dean and I were in a comfortable limbo; I had to tread lightly.

The subway car screeched to a stop at the next station and my destination was announced over the speakers. I erased the text and pocketed my phone as I stood to exit. The entire walk toward the park, I tried to conjure up excitement for my date with Carson. There was none. Absolutely none. Well, I did smell a pretzel stand, which caused me to salivate, but I couldn't really attribute that to Carson.

I was almost to the park, when I saw a sign for a new restaurant opening up across the street. I had a few minutes to spare, so instead of taking a right and crossing over toward the park, I waited for the light to change and jogged across the street to investigate. With any luck, I'd have a new restaurant to review soon. *Please be another crêperie, please be another crêperie.*

The restaurant was still in the construction phase, but the bare bones already hinted at how amazing it would be once they were finished.

I moved around to the front of the building to try to find more details when the name caught my attention. Ivy & Wine was painted in white across the brick, with the words "Coming Soon" beneath it. I squinted and read the name again, trying to draw out why the name seemed so familiar.

I stepped closer, inspecting the printed poster they'd taped to the front door. The owners of the restaurant had printed out a detailed menu so that pedestrians could start to get a feel for the place.

They boasted fresh flavors and seasonal dishes, but when I started to actually read the menu, I could feel the color drain my face. It was 100% identical to the menu Antonio Acosta had emailed us only a few days earlier. Every single detail, ingredient, and flavor paralleled ours, and when I scanned to the bottom where it listed the general manager's name, I knew who I had to blame.

Hunter was a little fucking rat.

CHAPTER THIRTY-EIGHT

DEAN

I PUSHED MY bike in through the back door and unclipped my helmet just as my front doorbell rang.

"I'm coming!" I yelled, annoyed at whoever kept ringing the bell. It was 8:00 PM on a Friday night; chances were I was about to be confronted by a Mormon missionary.

I propped my bike in the hallway and brushed the sweat from my brow just as Lily yelled through the door.

"Dean, hurry up! I know you're home!"

Lily?

I unlocked the door and pulled it open to find Lily standing on the other side with her hand poised, ready to keep knocking.

"Cool it, will you."

She groaned and pushed past me, nearly knocking me over. "Why don't you answer your phone?! I've called you ten times in the last twenty minutes!"

She was sweaty and breathing hard. Her cardigan was tied around her waist and her cotton dress was wrinkled. She bent over and rested her hands on her knees, trying to catch her breath.

"Did you run here?" I asked, furrowing my brows.

Her bright eyes landed on me with fury. "Of course I ran here! Hunter needs to be fired immediately!"

I held up my hands. "Slow down. Slow down. What's going on? Did he do something to you? Why aren't you on your date?"

She rolled her eyes and turned to the entryway table. She dumped her cardigan and her purse there and then reached in for her phone.

"I had to stand him up! I was on my way to my date when I noticed a restaurant under construction." She unlocked her phone and scrolled through pictures until she landed on one she was satisfied with. "This is the menu that was posted on the side of the building," she said, shoving the phone into my hand.

I zoomed in and squinted, trying to make out the small letters.

"Recognize anything? Oh, I don't know, maybe the entire thing?!"

I shook my head. "Are you certain? Maybe it just looks similar."

She laughed, clearly past the point of reason. "Scroll down and look who's listed as the general manager. Take a look at how loyal your employee is." She threw her hands into the air and stomped around the entryway. "I'm going to kill him. I'm going to drown him in the paella dish he STOLE from us!"

My hand clenched around her phone as I processed the information she'd just dumped on me. Hunter was working with another team, developing another restaurant across town with the menu and the vision we'd worked so hard to create.

It had been too easy for him to betray me. He had detailed summaries of everything from menu choices to color schemes. He had contact information for every single one of my contractors, vendors, and recruiters.

My blood started to boil. He thought he could get away with this? He thought he could sit in my office and feed me bullshit about a tough real estate market and expect me not to find out what he was really up to?

Lily's hand came into my line of sight and I realized she was trying to pry her phone from my grip before I crushed it.

"What are you going to do about it?" she asked, her voice much calmer now that I was the one losing my temper.

"I'll handle it," I said with a shake of my head.

She frowned. "What do you mean by that?"

I was already moving toward the kitchen, headed for the house phone hanging on the wall by the door. "I'm going to call my lawyer."

Her jaw dropped. "That's it?"

I was already dialing his number. "Intellectual property is tricky when it comes to restaurants that haven't even opened yet. He hasn't really broken any laws. Pursuing a civil case is the only way we can handle this. Just give me five minutes."

She took a seat at the kitchen table and crossed her arms, clearly annoyed with my lack of retribution. "He's such a slime ball. Y'know he hit on me again in Vegas too. He tried to get me to sneak off to a hotel room with him. God, I wish I'd punched him in the face then."

"Lily, calm down. We'll figure it out."

She nibbled on her bottom lip, too worked up to keep still.

"Dean," Mitch said, answering just before the call clicked over to voicemail. "This better be damn important. I was about to enjoy a meal at one of your damn restaurants."

"We have a situation."

He sighed. "Ah, hell. Hold on, let me go outside."

CHAPTER THIRTY-NINE

LILY

I PACED BACK and forth in the living room of my apartment. It was a small space, but I made do, huffing and puffing with annoyance as Jo sat watching me. I could feel her eyes volleying back and forth across the room, trying to keep up with my pace.

"If Dean says he's going to handle it, you should trust him," Jo said.

I shook my head. "No. His lawyer said that there wasn't much we could do. Dean didn't have that menu copyrighted. Trying to sue Hunter would cost Dean a fortune in legal fees and probably wouldn't result in any sort of solution."

"Maybe Dean could confront Hunter himself?"

I shot her a glare. "What? Like an old-fashioned duel?"

I was way past that point. I wanted Hunter to pay. I could handle his flirting and general incompetence, but this? It showed that there was more to the sweaty doofus exterior. He'd been playing us all along.

Jo crossed her arms. "Whatever. If his lawyer says there's nothing he can do, then you have to move on. You guys can just come up with a better menu or something."

I paused and turned to her. "Sweet, naive Jo. This isn't like fashion, where tastes change overnight."

She held up her hands for me to stop. "Oh god."

"You're insane if you think I'm going to let Hunter get away with this."

"Lily…" she warned.

If we couldn't sue him, I had to figure out how to convince Hunter to pull the plug on Ivy & Wine another way. Dean had already spoken with him, during Hunter's inevitable termination from employment. He didn't care that Dean had helped build his career. He didn't care that Dean had taught him everything he knew.

During the confrontation, Hunter showed no remorse and he admitted to nothing. He kept calling it a "disagreement", which was either to show that he was completely oblivious to the ridiculousness of such a statement, or to flaunt the fact that we couldn't touch him legally.

Fortunately for Dean, I wasn't going to let him get away with it.

I'd searched around online for any details concerning Ivy & Wine. A small NYC blog had posted a short snippet, but there was no mention of the investors or Hunter. Other than that, no other blogs had any details about the restaurant. I checked real estate and development websites to no avail. It wasn't until I searched the New York State Corporations Database that I got my first break. There was a registered agent listed under Ivy & Wine, LLC, one I wasn't expecting to find: Hunter's wife, Colette. *The wife he loves and respects oh so much.*

I searched around on Facebook, Twitter, and Instagram for any information I could find about Colette. From what little I could gather from digitally stalking her, she was a sweet woman from northern New York whose great-great-great-grandfather created the airplane or something. (*Okay, clearly I didn't read the whole article.*) All of her Facebook photos were of her and Hunter vacationing in the Hamptons and Cape Cod. She was from old money and Hunter owed every inch of his new restaurant to her. Meanwhile, he was traipsing around NYC humping anything that moved behind her back.

I just need proof...

I sat beside Josephine on the futon and angled my body toward her. "I think I have a plan, but I need your help."

She arched a brow. "With what?"

"How do you feel about going undercover?"

She dropped her head into her hands and groaned. "Please don't make me do something I'll regret."

● ● ●

Hunter's social media presence was nothing if not predictable. If there was something cool going on in the city, he had to tweet, blog, and post about how he was somehow involved. He was a "VIP" at every club in the city, he'd been to every bar opening this side of the Mississippi river, and he'd even once "sipped sizzurp with The Biebs #now-imabelieber". I nearly gouged my eyes out after reading that tweet.

Fortunately for me, his annoying need to brag about his adventures meant that I knew exactly where he planned to party on Friday night while his wife was out of town. His tweets leading up to the event read like this:

@BigGameHUNTER12334: Can't wait to party hard this Friday. #whenthewifeisawaythemicewillplay

@BigGameHUNTER12334: VIP 2Nite @OakBar #bottleservice #wheninrome

@BigGameHUNTER12334: We go hard #pregame #sippinondrank

And then of course, his wife had to chime in…

@Colletteinthecity: Don't have too much fun without me! ;)

@BigGameHUNTER12334: *kissy face*

Lord help us all.

Essentially he had the Twitter feed of a fourteen-year-old girl and the body of an overweight middle-aged man. He was basically begging for karma to bite him in the ass.

I closed Twitter and slid my phone into the small black backpack I'd picked out for the occasion. That, on top of my black beanie, black jeans, and a black long-sleeved shirt made me look less like a criminal and more like every other girl going out in the city on a Friday night. Hipster fashion really took the edge away from my badass vibe.

"Jo, you ready?" I yelled across the apartment.

She'd been fighting me on Operation Hunter Becomes the Hunted for the last two days, but there was no way around it. I couldn't be the bait for Hunter because he knew I hated him. He'd see right through the plan. Jo was my only option.

"Why do I have to wear this blonde wig? I look like

Shakira."

The blonde wig was partly for dramatic effect and partly because I knew Hunter liked blondes.

I rolled my eyes. "Let's not pretend your skinny ass has even half the hip action Shakira does. C'mon. Let me see it."

The bathroom door opened and Jo stepped out wearing our pre-planned outfit: a slinky red dress with matching heels. She looked sexy, and just a tad slutty—*perfect* for Hunter.

Jo propped her hand on her hip and shook her head. "This is such a terrible idea."

"No! It's brilliant. It's going to work." I paused. "Wait, you didn't tell Julian, right?"

"No, but I feel like I should. Isn't this technically cheating?"

I threw my hands up. "No! It's not like you're going to have sex with him or anything."

She blushed. "I don't know! You haven't exactly been forthcoming with me about all this."

"Okay. You're right. All I expect you to do is seduce Hunter and get him to admit all of his secrets so we can blackmail him."

She laughed. "Oh, that's all?"

I shrugged. "Let's make it hurt."

CHAPTER FORTY

LILY

IN THE MOVIES, they make the art of seduction seem simple. A pretty woman walks over to the target at the bar, he hits on her, bada bing bada boom, the FBI swoops in and deactivates the bomb, thus saving the world.

In reality, Jo wasn't a secret agent. Not even close. The world would have exploded like thirty minutes ago if the FBI were relying on her.

"I don't know. He seems busy. Maybe we should give him a few more minutes?" she asked, peering over her shoulder at Hunter for the thousandth time. I shook my head and took another sip of my water. I was purposely staying away from alcohol so I'd have my wits about me, but Jo was about to drive me to hard liquor.

"We've been here for an hour. Eventually you'll have to go talk to him."

"Or maybe we can scrap the plan and come up with something better. Maybe he didn't pay his taxes last year.

We could pretend to be the IRS."

I let my forehead fall to the bar as she continued to ramble.

"We say we're going to audit him and then we kidnap him. Julian has this spare room where we could keep him."

"Jo. Jo. Jo," I groaned, rocking my head back and forth across the bar. This was a complete waste of time and money.

"I'm not good at this sort of thing. Remember when the theater teacher, Mr. Finch, kicked me out of The Wizard of Oz in the seventh grade because I didn't act with enough soul?"

Oh Jesus.

I sat up and motioned to the bartender, prepared to scrap the plan all together, but then I smelled Hunter's spicy cologne. He approached the empty chair beside Jo and I froze.

"What's a girl like you doing sitting up here alone on a night like this at a bar?" he asked.

I had to bite my bottom lip to keep from laughing. He'd just jumbled about fourteen pickup lines together, hoping one of them would stick. I reached into the front pocket of my hoodie and pressed play on my tape recorder.

"Oh, uh…" Josephine fidgeted in her chair, unable to think of something charming to respond with. I kicked her foot and she giggled. "Just enjoying a drink."

"Is this your friend?" he asked, pointing to me.

I turned away so quickly that I nearly broke my neck. My blonde hair was tucked up under my beanie, but if he saw my face, he'd recognize me right away.

"Oh, her?" Josephine asked with a high-pitched voice. "She's just a, uh, a…one of those ladies from the local convent or something. She goes around to the bars to try to save souls."

"Is that so? Well I hope I don't see her at my bar, at the restaurant *I own*."

"Wow, you own a restaurant? That's so exciting!"

"It sure is sweetie. Hunter Smith, nice to meet ya," he oozed. "What are you drinking?"

She flinched back and her elbow collided with my spine.

"Ouch," I hissed, only loud enough for her to hear.

"Just a martini. Nothing special."

"Well I think a special lady like yourself deserves special attention. Why don't you come over to the booth with me and some friends? We have bottle service."

Yes. YES. This is what I needed.

She hesitated, fumbling for an excuse not to follow him, but then I delivered a highly discreet message through a series of coughs, sneezes, and sniffles. "Go." Cough. "With." Cough. "Him."

"What? Did the nun just say something?" Hunter asked.

Jo scooted her barstool back. "She's been saying it all night, 'go with *him*', meaning Jesus I guess. Let's get away from her."

I peered over my shoulder just in time to watch him lead her back to his corner of the bar. He put his hand on her lower back and she sidestepped away from him with a laugh. *Oh god.* I could only imagine the sort of drivel coming out of his mouth. Hopefully she'd managed to turn on her recorder before he dragged her off.

"You look like the president of the Dead Poets Society."

Motherfucker. I would have recognized that deep voice anywhere.

I turned to my left just as Dean took a seat at the bar beside me.

"What the hell are you doing here?" I asked, peering behind him for Julian. If he stomped over and punched Hunter in the face for flirting with Jo, my whole plan would be ruined.

"Josephine can't keep a secret," he said, waving down the bartender so he could order a drink.

That two-timing whoreface. She deserved to be Hunter's bait for the night.

"And?" I asked, scooting closer to him.

His brown eyes cut over to me and his lips curled up into a smirk. "And I'm going to help."

My jaw dropped. "Wait. Wait. You're not going to make me sit through some chastising speech about how I should have let you handle it?"

He laughed and turned to me. His knee brushed mine and his hand dropped to my thigh. I stared there as he continued, "I've been thinking a lot about what you said the other day. I've tried handling it my way and it didn't work. I'm willing to try your way now."

I nodded, completely in shock that he was on board with my plan. If I'd been a betting person, I'd have put a million dollars on Dean sabotaging the scheme. "So then where's your disguise?" I asked with a smirk.

"Ah," he said, dipping his free hand into the inside pocket of his suit jacket and extracting a small brown mustache.

I burst out laughing as he pressed it on above his upper lip. Beneath it, he was still as suave as ever: smooth, wavy hair, a clean-shaven jaw, and a fitted black suit. However, with the mustache in place, it was completely impossible to take him seriously.

"How do I look?" he asked.

I laughed. "You look like Tom Selleck."

He smiled, causing the mustache's cheap adhesive to fail on one side. "Did you come up with code names for the night?"

"Hmm, we could be Bonnie and Clyde," I suggested.

"A little too obvious."

I tapped my finger on the bar. "What about Sam and Frodo?"

He laughed. "You're Sam."

I smiled. "You know, some people think Sam and Frodo had a little thing going on while they were climbing those mountains. There were lots of lonely nights on the way to Mount Doom."

He curved his arm along the back of my chair and leaned forward so that his skewed mustache tickled the side of my face. "Frodo definitely had a thing for Sam."

I shivered and turned to kiss him, mustache and all, but then I noticed movement near Hunter's table out of the corner of my eye. I whipped my head in their direction, nearly falling off my barstool.

"Shit. They're leaving!" I hissed, reaching for my wallet so that I could close out our tab.

Dean let go of my leg and turned to the bar. "Go ahead. Follow them and I'll catch up."

I nodded and flew toward the entrance of the bar. "We'll meet again, Frodo!"

CHAPTER FORTY-ONE

DEAN

BY THE TIME I paid and walked out of Oak Bar, Lily, Hunter, and Josephine were nowhere in sight. I checked my phone and tried to call Lily, but she didn't answer. I scanned down the street in both directions, but they were gone. I ripped the cheap mustache from my upper lip and shoved it into my pocket just as my phone vibrated with a text.

> Lily: Can't talk. Hot on the trail.
> Dean: Lily, where are you guys??
> Lily: CODE NAME.

I growled though she couldn't hear it.

> Dean: SAM, which way did you head? Are you in a car or are you walking?
> Lily: oh no…

Dean: What??

A second later, my phone rang with a call from Lily.

"Can you hear me?" she whispered.

"Hardly. Where are you?"

I felt helpless standing in the middle of the sidewalk with nowhere to run. They could've been halfway across town already.

"Hunter and his friends just went into a place called Tease."

I groaned and took off running. Tease was just two blocks over from Oak Bar. If I ran, I could get there before Lily went inside.

"Lily. Wait for me to get there. Tease is a strip club and a sleazy one at that."

"What?" she yelled. "Josephine is in there with them!"

"Lily. Did you hear me? Do *not* go in without me."

When she didn't reply, I glanced at my phone and found the call had already ended. *Fuck.* I sped up and rounded the block. She wasn't going to listen to me and now she and Josephine were inside a shady strip club, all so Lily could carry out her half-baked plan to either ruin Hunter's restaurant, marriage, or both. The only reason I'd agreed to help was because I knew Lily wouldn't stop until Hunter paid. I should've known she wouldn't make it easy. *She never does.*

The bouncer guarding the door at Tease had beefy arms and a tiny head. The combination was unsettling, and when I tried to run past him, he held out his meat hook to stop me.

"What's the rush, buddy?" he asked.

I glanced down at his hand on my chest and then narrowed my eyes on him. "My friend is in there. I need to get her out."

He pursed his lips and shook his head. "Better not be talkin' 'bout a dancer. We don't need a jealous husband goin' in there and wreckin' business."

"She's not a dancer," I sneered, stepping back so his hand fell from my chest.

He studied me for another second and I clenched my fists. The longer I was out there talking to SmallHead McGee, the longer Josephine and Lily had to fend for themselves.

"There's a cover," he said, drawing out his words in a way that grated on my nerves.

I reached for my wallet. "Great. What is it?"

He cracked his fat knuckles. "For you?" He sized up my suit. "Thirty bucks."

That's it? He knew I needed to get in, he could have asked for any amount, and he'd come up with thirty dollars?

"All right, *buddy*," I said, throwing his word back at him and handing him forty dollars. "Keep the change."

He grinned as I walked through the door, staring down at the forty bucks like he'd just won the lottery.

The strip club was clouded with cigarette smoke and furniture straight out of the 80s. Red vinyl chairs rimmed three separate stages, a large one in the center and two smaller ones that flanked it on either side. Red and yellow lights flickered overhead, illuminating the girls dancing on each one. They were the afternoon crew, the stragglers, the dancers that had no dance left in them. They looked like they needed a week's vacation and a few less days spent inside the tanning bed.

"Awww yeah. *Yeah. Yeah.* That's right guys, it's free steak night tonight at Teeeeeeeeeeease." The emcee boomed over the speakers. "Get yourself a plate and get that green ready for our next dancer. Up next on the main stage is Dusty Rooooooose. Dusty Rose is a fan favorite, so you'll want to move in close, but not too close! She's been known to biiiiiiiiiiite." I resisted the urge to roll my eyes. "Please put your hands together and give a warm welcome to Ms. Dusty Rose!"

Loud pop music started streaming through the speakers as Dusty Rose took the stage in a bright pink shirt and a short plaid skirt. She looked to be in her forties, tanned and tired, but she was wearing her bleached hair in short pigtails and dancing to old Britney Spears like she was twenty-one again.

I scanned the crowd for Lily, but she was impossible to find in the dim lighting. A waitress in a short glittery dress sidled up beside me, running her hand up my side. "Thirsty, big boy?" she cooed.

I shook my head. "Did you see two girls come in just a second ago? Two blondes?"

She smiled up at me, stringing a finger through her hair and twisting it around. "Sure I wasn't one of them?"

Clearly, she wasn't going to help.

I made to move past her and she reached out for my arm. "Fine. Jeez, you're no fun. I'm pretty sure one of them is over on the other side of the bar."

"And the other?" I asked.

She smirked and tilted her head toward Dusty Rose. "She's backstage."

CHAPTER FORTY-TWO

LILY

I HAD ASSUMED that New York City would offer me some pretty eye-opening experiences. I'd planned on visiting the great museums and rifling through independent bookstores in Brooklyn. I'd had hopes of sampling the best cuisine the city had to offer and then lying beneath the oak trees of Central Park, dreaming of the fancy cuisine I'd devour the next day.

Instead, I found myself backstage at a squalid strip club, weaving in and out of dancers. In my imagined life, my hair blew in the breeze on the Hudson Bay. In real life, it stank of cigarette smoke. In my imagined life, I mingled with the movers and shakers of the culinary capital of the world. In real life, I was colliding with coke-fueled women who'd run out of options.

When I'd walked into the club, Hunter had been hovering near the entrance, trying to find a spot to claim. He'd spun in a circle with Josephine by his side, inspecting the room for open tables. He'd been seconds away from landing on the spot where I stood frozen and I'd reacted just in time, slipping behind the black curtain with hopes that it lead to a bathroom or storage closet. Instead, I found myself backstage.

I coughed and waved my hand in front of my face, hoping to clear the air. It was no use. Smoke, hair spray, and perfume blended together into a watery eye inducing cloud. I blinked away the haze and glanced down at my phone. Jo was ignoring me, most likely deciding if she was going to suffocate me or throw me out the window later. I'd told her we had to follow Hunter into a bar, not a strip club. I was discovering along with her how big a difference there was.

Lily: JO. Are you okay? ANSWER ME.

I tried again.

Lily: Do you want to leave? This is stupid. Let's go!

I was about to head back out through the door and break our cover when she finally texted me back.

Jo: He's drunk and I know I almost have him! Just stay hidden.

"What are you doing back here, sugar?"

I turned to my left to find a half-naked dancer pulling her uniform on over her head. It looked like a cheap Halloween costume. She was meant to be a cop with a badge that read "Sergeant Sexy" in glittery letters. Her dark skin was coated with sparkly lotion and her hair was twisted into tight curls. She had the biggest pair of boobs I'd ever seen in real life and for a moment I couldn't even answer her question because I was too mesmerized by the sight of them.

"Sugar?" she asked again.

I stared up into her honey brown eyes. "I'm spying."

She laughed. "On your baby daddy? That never ends well." She tsked and turned around. "Zip me up, will ya?"

She sucked in as much as possible and I stepped forward to zip her up. The dress was so tight she'd have to cut herself out of it at the end of the night.

"I'm not spying on a man. I'm here for a friend."

She turned back around and gave me a onceover. Something told me she didn't believe me about spying for a friend, but she shrugged anyway. "There's a spot between the main stage and the left side stage where you can pull the curtain back and peek through. Don't be stupid about it though. Big Ronnie'll chew me out if he finds ya."

Before I could say thanks, she spun away, dancing to music I couldn't hear. Her hips swayed side to side and she arched her back, dragging her left hand down her right arm. It was a routine, *her* routine.

I walked closer to the curtain and started gently pulling back sections, looking for an opening. I kept waiting for one of the other dancers to stop me, but everyone was too busy getting ready to notice the weird girl in the beanie.

Before I could find a gap in the curtain, my phone buzzed with two text messages.

Dean: Are you backstage??

Jo: I GOT IT. He just sang like a canary and I recorded it all. He's throwing up in the bathroom. Meet

208

me at the front door.

I pumped my fist in the air. *We did it!* Hunter was going down and I hadn't subjected Jo to a strip club for nothing. Win win. I was going to celebrate with Dean and bask in his compliments of what a good sleuth I was.

"Hey! Step off, bitch," a dancer said, interrupting the party in my head.

I'd been too preoccupied to see her leave the stage and when I'd fist-pumped, I'd narrowly missed punching her in the face. She reared back and pushed me before I could explain the mistake.

I lost my footing and tumbled back, grasping onto the black curtain like it was going to catch my fall. In reality, the thin material gave way beneath my weight and my butt hit the stage with too much momentum to stop. I rolled back—clinging to the one gymnastics lesson I'd had at age five—and landed on my stomach, flat on the center stage with bright red light shining down on me.

Oh shit.

"Looks like we have a surprise guest on the stage now folks," the MC said, stalling. "Kimmy Cat was supposed to be up next, but let's see where this goes."

I caught movement out of the corner of my eye and watched as two bouncers made their way toward the stage with angry scowls aimed at me.

I surveyed the crowd around me. They weren't angry, they were confused. I pushed onto the heels of my feet and tried to regain my equilibrium.

One of the bouncers reached the stage and leaned in to grab my arm.

"Let her dance!" a customer yelled.

"Yeah! Let her dance! Let her dance!" another chanted.

They want me to dance.

THEY WANT ME TO DANCE.

"Ladddiesss and gentlemen, we've got a brand new dancer on the stage tonight!" the emcee began, trying to make sense of the situation.

Oh no. No, no, no.

I stood and tried to get the emcee's attention. I waved my hands back and forth in front of my chest in a universal sign of "STOP. LET ME OFF THIS STRIP CLUB STAGE."

"Looks like we have a...sexy ninja," he improved, misinterpreting my signals for dance moves. "Maybe a slutty samurai, showing off her erotic moooooooves! Give it up for, uh..."

"Busty Black Belt!" Josephine yelled from somewhere in the back of the crowd.

"Buuuuuuusty Black Belt!" he echoed, changing songs to T-Pain's "I'm in Love With a Stripper".

I smiled and held my hand over my brow to find Josephine, but the lights were blinding. I could only see the first row of men, smiling and goading me to dance.

"Show us what you got, honey," a guy yelled from the front row.

I stood in the center of the stage, completely frozen. I had two options: I could dance or I could let the bouncers drag me away.

"Work it, baby," another guy yelled.

My cheeks flamed as I wrestled with indecision, but in the end, my body made up my mind for me. It started moving to the beat, slowly at first, just my head and shoulders rocking back and forth. The front row of men cheered me on and I smiled.

This isn't so bad.

The emcee kicked the music up another notch, loud enough to drown out the sounds of the club. I tried to shimmy to the left and to the right, but I couldn't quite work out how to coordinate my chest, shoulders, and feet.

"Sexier, honey!"

They wanted sexy? I'd show 'em sexy. My rolodex was chock-full of the most sultry dance moves: stirring the pot, grocery shopping, watering the lawn, you named it. I watered that lawn like my life depended on it and the crowd sat stunned, watching me in complete silence.

I pulled the beanie from my head and tossed it out into the crowd. That earned me a few whistles and that's when I saw Dean standing at the end of the stage with his arms crossed. His features were cast in shadows, but I could see the incredulous grin stretched across his lips as he watched me.

I bit down on my bottom lip to keep from laughing, and the crowd went wild.

"Yeahhh, honey!"

"Keep biting your lip!"

Dean tilted his head to the right and I glanced over to see the pole gleaming under the neon lights. I hadn't touched it yet, but I knew I would before the song finished. I shimmied to the back of the stage and tried to recall how dancers usually mounted the poles in movies. *Do they just hop on, or do they get a running start first?* It felt like I needed a running start, so I let T-Pain's wise, auto-tuned words wash over me as I ran straight for it. My body collided with the metal and I clung onto it like a baby monkey grabbing on to a tree branch. Usually the dancers jumped on and started to spin, but I just slowly slid down the greasy pole until my butt hit the floor. Nothing happened. The song ended and I was left with absolute silence.

One slow clap started near the back and then the emcee spoke up halfheartedly, "Well, A for effort, right folks?"

Josephine whooped it up beside Dean, tossing dollars onto the stage. "THAT'S MY BEST FRIEND!" she yelled.

The two bouncers who had stood off to the side during my "performance" stepped forward as I uncoiled my legs from the base of the pole, but Dean got to me before they did. He reached up to help me down from the stage.

"That was amazing, I ca—" he began.

Hunter emerged through the crowd, having left the bathroom sometime during my performance. He limped through the crowd, clearly looking worse for wear.

"Hey!" he bellowed, squinting quizzically toward the stage.

We all froze, getting ready to run in case he identified us through the dim haze.

"Why the hell was the nun dancing onstage?"

CHAPTER FORTY-THREE

DEAN

"YOU GUYS DID all of this tonight? While I was at dinner with my sister?" Julian asked, holding Dean's limp mustache and staring at the three of us with a dropped jaw.

Lily shrugged. "I mean, it took some planning."

Josephine tried to sidle closer to him, but he shot her a warning glance with narrowed eyes. "And you didn't even think to tell me?"

She nibbled on her bottom lip, trying to come up with an excuse. "I knew you wouldn't be okay with it."

He grunted. "Well yeah, you don't know what a guy like that might've done if he'd found you out."

"I was there," I said, handing Julian the three fingers of bourbon I'd just poured for him. "Hunter was a harmless drunk and she was safe the whole time."

It was a white lie. A harmless lie. We were all safely inside my house, so what did it matter if an hour earlier Josephine had been alone with Hunter inside a strip club?

Julian didn't need to know every gritty detail.

Julian stared down at the blonde wig laying across Josephine's lap. "So did it work?"

I smirked and pointed to the recorder beside Jo. "Play the recording for him."

We had over an hour of Hunter's drunk ramblings at the strip club. We'd listened to it all earlier, but we only played the highlights back for Julian.

At five minutes into the recording, Hunter started bragging about his new restaurant: *"It's gonna be the hottest restaurant in New York."*

Then there was another ten minutes of him drunkenly bragging about his "brilliant" idea. Jo fast-forwarded to get to the good stuff: Colette.

"Aren't you married?"

"Only on paper, baby."

"What does that mean?"

"It means that when she's out of town, I do whatever I want, and tonight, I think that'll be you."

Julian held up his hand and Josephine hit pause. "All right, all right, I get it. You have some dirt on him. Now what are you going to do?"

"I just left a message for him to meet me here tomorrow. I'll confront him with the recording and let him decide his own fate," I said.

"What if he doesn't back down? What if he doesn't care about his wife hearing it?" Jo asked.

I shrugged. "That's the beauty of Lily's plan. It's irrelevant what he thinks, because we can always just send the recording to his wife. I don't think Mrs. Moneybags will be so forgiving. So he either does what we say and kills the restaurant himself, or he loses it completely."

Julian slung back the rest of his bourbon and set the

glass down on the coffee table in front of Lily. "Brilliant, but that's enough cloak-and-dagger for me for one night. Jo, you ready to go? I'm exhausted."

She pushed up off the couch and took his hand.

"You still smell like Hunter," he said, wrapping an arm around her.

"He didn't even touch me. I just smell like the smoke from the strip club."

His paused. "Wait, you guys were at a strip club?"

Lily hopped to her feet and ushered them out into the foyer. "All right well, have a good night guys! Julian, you should know that she only went along with this as a favor to me." She held up the blonde wig. "As repayment, I'll let y'all keep this. I'm sure you two can find *some* use for it."

At first he kept his straight face, ignored Lily, and ushered Josephine over the threshold. The door had almost closed behind them when there was a pause. Julian's hand slipped back through the crack and Lily dropped the wig into it. Then, without a word, he shut the door.

"Knew he'd take it."

Lily locked the door behind them and propped her back against it. She'd left her black beanie at the club. Her blonde hair was parted down the middle, falling down over her shoulders. Her tight black shirt had ridden up on the left side, revealing a little sliver of tan skin above her jeans. That patch of skin called to me. I dropped my glass on the table in the foyer and moved closer.

"Do I still smell like smoke too?" she asked as I wrapped my hands around her waist. I dipped down and buried my face in her hair. It smelled like her shampoo, a tropical scent filled with coconuts and sea breeze.

"You smell like Lily."

She smiled against my neck and then her tongue slipped

out and licked down my skin.

"You taste like Dean."

I laughed and stepped back, forcing her along with me. We made it up to my bedroom slowly, pausing along the way so that she could tear off my shirt in the hallway. I stripped off her jeans on the stairs and she straddled me in the doorway to my bedroom, curving her hips against me until I lost track of where I was going. We were supposed to head into my bathroom and shower the strip club off us, but instead, I carried her to my bed and we fell back onto the comforter.

No one had control of me the way Lily did. I laid back on my bed as she rolled on top of me, her hair tickling my chest. She was a force of nature, a swirling tornado that made me feel weightless and free one minute, and slammed into a tree trunk at 130 miles per hour the next. I let her hold my hands to the side. I let her think she had control for once. I had a dopey smirk on my face as she kissed her way down my chest. Inside, my heart rioted, warning me to proceed with caution.

This was dangerous.

She was dangerous.

"Dean?" she asked, staring up at me with her honey brown eyes. "I'm really happy you were there tonight, helping me."

She was opening up to me, confirming with her words what she was showing me with her body.

"We make the perfect team," she said softly.

I could handle the Tiger Lily, the fierce, independent woman who fought with me every inch of the way—but this? The vulnerable girl opening up to me as she lay naked across my chest?

She scared the shit out of me.

I had goals. I had restaurants to open. I had Forbe's lists to top, and Lily would get in the way of that. Lily wouldn't be an easy addition to my life. She wouldn't appreciate the time I gave her. She'd demand all of me, every ounce, siphoning my focus away from my work until I resented her for it.

Love changes a person. I couldn't let Lily slip into my life and change the core of me. The need for more was always there, lingering in the periphery of my mind. When I took a long lunch or slept fifteen minutes past my alarm, I pushed myself harder to make up for lost time. I had the world to conquer and Lily would only stand in the way of that.

● ● ●

I took my time showering, trying to gather up the wits Lily had stolen over the last hour and a half. The water steamed up, burning the skin across my shoulder blades, but I relished the sensation until the water ran cold. Only then did I step out and wrap the towel around my waist.

I wiped my hand across the fogged glass and met Lily's gaze in the mirror. I wanted more time away from her, more time to regroup.

She was standing at the door of the bathroom, holding up a gold-leafed invitation with one hand and clutching her towel across her body with the other.

"What's this?" she asked, turning it over in her hand.

It was an invitation to the James Beard Awards, essentially the Oscars of the food world. I'd worked my ass off for years to be noticed in the community and finally, for the first time, I was nominated for an award: Outstanding

Restaurateur. Just to be nominated was an honor beyond anything I could comprehend, but I'd held the achievement close to my heart.

A nomination wasn't a win.

"It's an invitation to the James Beard Awards," I said, reaching for my toothbrush.

Her eyes widened and her grasp on the invitation tightened. *She knows how important the ceremony is.* "It's next week and you haven't returned your RSVP."

I shrugged. "I don't think they'll mind. I'm a guest of honor."

She carried the invitation in and set it down on the bathroom counter, meeting my eye in the mirror.

"You want me to fill it out for us and send it in?"

For us.

Lily took that blank card and filled it in for herself. She assumed I would take her because she thought we were a team; she'd said so herself. I looked up in the mirror and saw her eyes brimming over with hope for *us;* I couldn't mimic her sentiment. Where she felt hope, I only felt fear.

"I'm going alone."

CHAPTER FORTY-FOUR

LILY

MY FACE STUNG as if he'd slapped me. I held my hand up to my cheek, just to check, but there was no pain, only red hot heat. The blotchy blush spread from my cheeks down over my neck as Dean stood with his back to me, meeting my eyes in the mirror and daring me to push him on his comment.

I stood there in *his* towel, on *his* cold tile floor. I was naked with the scent of *his* body wash swirling up around me. I turned on my heel and found my jeans, pulling them on before I could find my underwear. I slipped on my bra and tugged my shirt back in place. My hair was still sopping wet and it seeped down the back of my black t-shirt, chilling me to the bone.

Dean came to stand at the door of his bathroom with his towel hung low on his hips. He crossed his arms and turned his dark eyes on me. In the light, when the sun caught them, his eyes turned a golden brown, so bright that I had to look away. In that moment, in the dim light of his room, they were dark pools of black, emotionless and cold.

"Lily, we're making this up as we go along. I never made you any promises. You said it yourself, this thing between us is just sex."

His voice sounded dead and my eyes stung with unshed tears.

I didn't want him to speak and I sure as shit didn't want to hear his explanations.

"You'll find a better man than me."

I stared at the ground and blinked away the tears threatening to spill.

"You think this is a life, Dean? You think those restaurants will make you happy? One day you'll wake up and realize that you're completely alone, and your insides will twist with regret. No man is an island. *Not even you.*"

I stepped toward him and pointed my finger at his chest. His jaw tightened, but he held his ground, committed to his decision.

"And you know what? I'll have moved on. I'm not waiting around for you, Dean Harper. I'm not begging you to change or standing by as you pretend the past few weeks haven't been the best weeks of your life. Challenging, yes, but don't tell me that you'd trade them. So have fun at your awards ceremony. I'm sure it'll feel good to stand on that stage alone with a bunch of strangers clapping for you."

I turned away and he stayed in that doorway. I walked out of his room, down the stairs, and out the front door, and he stood still, watching me walk out of his life like it was the easiest thing he'd ever done.

I held onto the fact that I hadn't cried in front of him. I convinced myself that the insults I'd flung had been well-worded. I wanted my barbed words to sink deep and fester inside him. I still had a thousand things I wanted to yell, but it was done. Dean was in his house and I was walking home alone with wet hair and wet cheeks. I skipped the subway and ignored the cabs. I walked until my feet hurt and I used the burn in my legs to distract me from the burn in my heart.

My phone was silent the entire way home. No text messages, no phone calls. Dean didn't run out after me and he didn't care enough to know if I made it home okay.

I was relieved to find the apartment empty. I tore at my clothes, tossing them into the trash on the way to the bathroom. They were sweaty and filled with memories I wanted erased by the morning. I turned on the shower and stepped inside. I squeezed shampoo over my scalp once, and then again, trying to expunge the scent of Dean.

I lathered myself in body wash from the top of my head to the tips of my toes and let it linger before washing it away with scalding water. I brought my arm to my nose and sniffed, feeling my heart break when I still smelled him there. His masculine scent overpowered my flowery body wash. I cried and scraped at my skin, sliding down to the floor of the shower. My fingers scrubbed furiously as I let his words haunt me.

I never made you any promises.

For all the progress we'd made, he still treated us like a contract that hadn't been signed. I cried and let the water blend with my tears. The salty mixture disappeared past my lips as I curled into a ball.

I just wanted to get his scent off me.

I wanted to get him off me.

I wanted him *gone*.

CHAPTER FORTY-FIVE

DEAN

I LET LILY walk out of my apartment and I stood there frozen. I was pushing her away for good; I knew it, and I couldn't stop myself. Lily was a distraction at best and a liability at worst. I would have picked up on cues that something was amiss with Hunter had Lily not soaked up my attention during staff meetings. Looking back, there'd been plenty of signs that Hunter had been up to no good. It had worked out in the end, but I wasn't going to make the same mistake twice. For the time being, my focus would remain on work.

● ● ●

Lily had walked out of my life the week before and I'd gotten more work done in those seven days than I had in months. I'd worked late every night and I'd have continued on like that forever, but the James Beard Awards wasn't an event to skip. Every top chef, restaurateur, food critic, and journalist was in attendance, crammed into small red velvet seats awaiting the moment when the awards ceremony gave way to the cocktail hour. We'd all stand around for an hour or two ass-kissing the hell out of anyone we could manage to snag a minute with, but hopefully I'd be wearing a James Beard medal around my neck as I did it.

We'd already suffered through most of the awards, shit like Outstanding Baker and Outstanding Wine Program. I fidgeted in my seat and ignored the two guests seated beside me. According to the program, my award was next, and suddenly it was impossible to sit still.

A beautiful woman with dark, exotic features stepped out onto the stage to announce the nominees. I vaguely recognized her from a cooking show, but there were too many to keep track of to know for sure. She stood behind the mic with a gold-leafed envelope clutched beneath her bright red nails.

"The nominees for the James Beard Award for Outstanding Restaurateur are three individuals that each have a finger on the pulse of American cuisine. These three nominees have set high national standards in restaurant operations and entrepreneurship."

I straightened my bowtie and leaned forward in my seat. I knew the cameramen would flash my face across the giant screens flanking the stage, but I didn't paste on a fake smile. I was too focused on the announcer's words.

"Our first nominee is Rob Villarreal. Rob has opened countless successful restaurants in the heart of Seattle. His restaurants are youthful and full of the spirit of the city."

Rob Villareal had invested in Starbucks early and used his money to open shitty restaurants. If he won, I'd never drink Starbucks again.

"Our second nominee, Victor Keller, has established himself as the restaurant god of Las Vegas. He operates five restaurants along the Strip, one of which, La Viva, has placed in the top fifty restaurants in the world three years in a row."

Victor Keller was a hack. He had his nose so far up the ass of the restaurant world it was a wonder he hadn't shown up at the awards with pink eye.

"Our final nominee, Dean Harper is an up-and-coming restaurateur, making his mark in New York City one inventive restaurant at a time. In a climate where most restaurants rely on stifling traditions or flashy gimmicks, he focuses on fresh, innovative flavors and contemporary designs to set his restaurants apart from the competition."

My heart was beating out of my chest as she ripped open that envelope. I wanted to grip someone's hand, but the Asian mom to my left was staring down at her program, and the man to my right was too busy checking his iPhone to notice my nerves.

"And the winner of the James Beard Award for Outstanding Restaurateur goes to…" She smiled and paused to make eye contact with the audience. I was going to have a heart attack if she didn't say the name soon. "Dean Harper! The youngest winner of the Outstanding Restaurateur award in history!"

I blinked.

And blinked again.

I squeezed my hands into fists and sat frozen.

The camera zoomed in on my face so that everyone in the opera house got an up-close view of my wide eyes. I was stunned and there was no one to push me up out of my seat or kiss my cheek as I made my way to the stage.

I stood and slipped past the attendees in my row. A few of them clapped me on the shoulder, but no one offered actual words of encouragement. I walked up the stairs on the side of the stage and was met by a young man waiting to put the heavy silver medal around my neck. My hands shook and my brow beaded with sweat as the magnitude of the achievement set in. I was the youngest winner of the award. *I am the youngest, most successful restaurateur in the United States.* I swallowed down that lump of success. The award was everything I'd worked toward since leaving my family in Iowa. It was the pinnacle of success and as I bent down to let the young man slip the medal around my neck, I stared down at the black stage and focused on the one emotion overpowering all the others: regret.

I cleared my throat and spoke into the mic, squinting at the glare of the lights beaming down on me.

"This award is a recognition of culinary accomplishment, not speechmaking ability, so I'll keep this short."

The crowd laughed good-naturedly.

"I never thought I'd find great success in a market like New York City. I fought tooth and nail for the top chefs and the best people. In the end, I look back on those long nights and lost weekends and I can honestly say…"

I paused and looked down at my medal, glowing in the opera house lights, and I felt my voice start to quake. I tried to clear my throat again. "I can honestly say…"

It *wasn't* worth it.

None of it was worth it.

I took a step back, met the crowd's gaze, and left my sentence hanging. "Thank you."

The crowd didn't clap right away; they were waiting for the second half of my sentence, but it never came.

Eventually, after a long pause, the orchestra started playing and the opera house welled with light, happy music. I turned and let the presenter usher me backstage. She was busy congratulating me and gushing about how excited I must feel. I wanted to shake off the grip she had on my shoulder. I wanted her to leave me be so I could have one second to realize that where I should have felt absolute happiness, I only felt sorrow. It felt like I'd been punched in the stomach and the feeling wasn't fading.

The threat of tears forced me to the bathroom back stage. I played it off like I was overwhelmed with the award and no one bothered me. No one thought twice about the emotional man with his shiny-ass medal and his rapidly closing throat.

I propped my hands on the bathroom counter and the medal clanged against the granite. None of it made sense. The out-of-control feeling I'd had the last night I was with Lily was supposed to have disappeared the moment I pushed her out of my life. The idea was simple: I'd felt like I was in the driver's seat before her, so once I pushed her away and she was gone, I'd regain that control.

"Crazy feeling, isn't it?"

I looked up to see an older man in a fitted tuxedo washing his hands in the sink beside me. He also wore a James Beard medal around his neck and I recognized him as the winner of the Outstanding Chef award.

"Yeah, crazy."

He smiled.

"Family here tonight?" I asked.

His brow furrowed for a moment and then he met my gaze in the mirror. "No. They stayed behind in England when I moved to the States for work a few years ago."

"Don't you miss them?"

"I'm sure you understand better than anyone," he replied. "The culinary world is not a field for those who want a picket fence and two and a half kids. We work nights and weekends and our days are spent dreaming up the next great idea. There's not time for much else."

He smiled as if he was proud of the man he was, the man who would leave his family to pursue his own selfish dreams. I'd thought I wanted to be a man like him, but my life wouldn't be wasted in the back offices of a bustling restaurant.

Not any more.

When I walked out of the bathroom a few minutes later, I felt lighter than I had in years. I'd left the weight of the medal on the bathroom sink, and the weight of former dreams alongside it.

CHAPTER FORTY-SIX

LILY

I HAD TOO much pride to call Dean, but I loved him enough to con my way into his dumb awards ceremony. I leaned against the back wall, out of everyone's way as the skinny bitch on stage read through the descriptions for the three nominees. I thought she smiled extra wide as she read off Dean's accomplishments, but I was too far away to know for sure. With a flick of her wrist, she tore into the envelope and I held my breath. I wanted him to win. I hated him with every bone in my body, but I wanted him to win.

"Dean Harper! The youngest winner of the Outstanding Restaurateur award in history!"

He was so shocked and so handsome and so alone as he took that stage. My heart sank as he gripped the medal in his hand. He should have been elated, but his voice sounded flat over the mic, like he was reading off a farewell speech at a funeral. I nibbled on my bottom lip. I didn't want to be right about what I'd told Dean—that he was alone, that no one would be there to congratulate him or hold his hand. I'd yelled that at him during a moment of fury, but now my words were coming true. Dean had no one to congratulate him. No one that mattered.

He offered the crowd a small, tight smile and then walked off stage after the shortest speech of the night. The pretty announcer trailed after him, trying to keep up with his quick pace. He disappeared behind the stage and I moved to follow after him. I was in a floor-length gown I'd borrowed from Jo, and I'd spared the time to do my hair and makeup. No one batted an eyelash at me as I swept the curtain aside and stepped into the depths of the opera house. The belly of the building was nothing compared to the ornate detailing in the auditorium. Backstage consisted of a narrow black hallway branching off to separate rooms every few feet. One sign pointed me in the direction of the stage and another directed me to a women's changing room. I passed a few nondescript black doors and then I heard Dean's voice over the sound of running water.

Another voice seeped through the door, but I couldn't make out the conversation. I pushed my ear to the door and tried in vain to hear through the thick wood. It was no use—unless, of course, they were actually saying "geri hrjt hempjrh ggfffnj." In which case, I could hear them perfectly.

A moment later, the water cut off and footsteps echoed on the other side of the door. The handle turned and the door swung out. I jumped, swiveled, and tried to flatten my body against the wall like a pancake, but the door came straight for me. I held my foot out and caught it just before it broke my face.

Dean's cologne hit me first, rolling a wave of nostalgia over me. The last night I'd slept with him, he'd pinned me

229

to his bed with his face pressed to the crook of my neck. We were so close it was suffocating and I'd inhaled deeply, filling my lungs with the scent of him until it overwhelmed me. Maybe if I'd known that would be my last night in his bed, I would have breathed in a little deeper, tried to fill my lungs until they burned.

His profile slipped past me and I caught sight of his strong jaw, straight nose, and furrowed brows. He was a vision in his black tuxedo. His broad shoulders filled out the jacket and his black pants tapered down his long legs.

He didn't see me as he passed. He was already halfway down the hallway by the time the door fell closed with a heavy thud.

It was a few minutes later, as I told myself I had to move, that I realized his chest had been bare.

He'd left the medal in the bathroom.

Why?

CHAPTER FORTY-SEVEN

From: Dean Harper
To: Lily Black, Julian Lefray, Zoe Davis
Subject: Ivy & Wine

Seems Hunter retired from the restaurant world for good. I put in an offer on the building where he was planning to open Ivy & Wine. The construction team is already halfway through building the restaurant we designed. Maybe we should send him a thank you basket?

D. Harper

From: Julian Lefray
To: Lily Black, Dean Harper, Zoe Davis
Subject: Re: Ivy & Wine

Wow. Lily's plan actually worked. And all it took was

turning my girlfriend into an escort! ;)

-J

From: Zoe Davis
To: Lily Black, Dean Harper, Julian Lefray
Subject: Re: Re: Ivy & Wine

I just went by the building!!!! Hunter actually ended up helping us a ton. That space will be finished in a few months. If we buckle down we could open early next year.

Zoe

From: Dean Harper
To: Lily Black, Julian Lefray, Zoe Davis
Subject: Re: Re: Re: Ivy & Wine

Is everyone available to meet this week? I have a list two miles long of shit we need to get done.

D. Harper

From: Lily Black
To: Julian Lefray, Zoe Davis, Dean Harper
Subject: Re: Re: Re: Re: Ivy & Wine

Glad we got the space. I'm under the weather, so could someone take notes and email me what y'all discuss at the meeting? Thanks.

-Lily Black

● ● ●

LILY

"PRETENDING YOU'RE SICK so you don't have to see Dean will only work for a few days," Josephine said as she pushed off the back of the futon. I slammed my laptop closed and shot her a glare.

"Jeez. Snoop much?"

She shrugged and went back to the kitchen, where she was halfway finished making a peanut butter and jelly sandwich. Apparently my typing had distracted her from her lunch.

"Julian says Dean is—"

I held up my hand to silence her. "I don't care what Julian says Dean is. I don't care if Dean is dating Miley Cyrus or jumping off skyscrapers because he wants to win me back. I. Don't. Care."

She smirked and eyed me over the jar of peanut butter. "I don't think suicide is the best avenue for regaining your affection. It's kind of counterproductive, don't you think?"

I groaned and slid down so I could shove my head beneath the pillows. "Please stop talking about Dean! Do I need to remind you about the Dean Jar again?"

She laughed and I knew she was glancing over at the giant empty cheese puff container I'd labeled "DEAN JAR" a few days ago. It worked like a swear jar:

$1: Referring to the likeness of Dean in a way.

$2: Discussing Dean in this apartment.

$5: Making me watch a TV show with an actor who looks remotely like Dean. Examples include: Men with blond hair. Men who wear suits. Men who live in New York City. Men who are lovable in a rough-around-the-edges sort of way.

$1,000,000: Saying shit like "Let me set you up with someone." I don't want to date. I want to stab someone. If you set me up with a man, I will stab him. His blood will be on your hands.

I was planning on using the money raised to buy a swimming pool full of ice cream.

"I see you added a new one to the list today," she said, walking around the futon and pushing my legs aside so that she could sit down.

$0.50: Using words that start with the letter "D".

"Yes and you've already broken it quite a few times," I groaned, reaching for her purse. "It's not that hard, Jo."

"You don't think you're asking a little too much of me?"

"Jo, I don't expect you to understand. You're basically living out a Lifetime movie with Julian. You live in a magical fairy world where real problems don't exist."

"That's not true. Just this morning, a bug flew up my nose as I was walking to work."

"Did you just make that up?"

"Want a bite of my sandwich?" she asked, changing the subject.

"Yeah."

"Should I just shove it under the pillow and assume you'll find it?"

"Yeah."

I chewed on a bite of the sandwich she slipped under the pillow for me. It was soft and simple and reminded me of my childhood. After slipping me another bite, Jo spoke up. "Are you still wearing his medal?"

The futon's cushion pressed the cold medal against my chest. It was heavy and unwieldy and I wore it every day, like an albatross. I'd nabbed it from the opera house bathroom with the intention of giving it back to him— surely, he hadn't meant to leave it behind—but then I'd slipped it around my neck and the weight had felt good. The medal represented everything Dean had struggled for in life and when I wore it, I pretended that included me.

"I'm not *not* wearing his medal, if that's what you're asking."

"Lil, we need to set you up with someone already, just to get you focused on someone new."

"YES!" I cried.

"Really? You want me to find someone?"

"Of course not, but I can finally afford my pool!"

CHAPTER FORTY-EIGHT

DEAN

JULIAN AND I were halfway through a Saturday morning bike ride when his phone rang. He waved me over to the side of the road. We hopped up onto the sidewalk and I pulled out my water bottle, guzzling down half of it while he spoke on the phone.

"Yeah, I can be there in a second," he said. "I'm actually biking right by your place now."

He flashed me an apologetic smile, but I shrugged him off. If it weren't for Julian, I'd have been working my way through a pile of building plans.

"We need to pause the ride?" I asked as he hung up.

He nodded. "Josephine wants me to come take a look at their dishwasher before she calls in a maintenance request."

I smirked. "You ever fix a dishwasher before?"

He laughed and hopped back onto his bike. "Never. My plan is to bang on it a few times and then tell her to call in the request."

I shook my head and pulled out onto the road after him. He stood and pedaled fast to set our pace and I raced after him, appreciating the lack of weekday traffic. By the time we reached Josephine's apartment complex, my legs were on fire.

I locked my bike up beside Julian's and thought of Lily. It was a maddening game, trying to convince myself that she and I were over. I knew I'd ruined it. It'd taken so long to peel back her stubborn, annoying, controlling layers so that I could catch even a single glimpse of her vulnerable side, and in that same night, I'd taken whatever measly amount of trust I'd earned and tossed it out the window.

She wouldn't give me a second chance. Lily was too smart to waste her time on a guy who didn't have his priorities in order.

I followed Julian up the stairs to their apartment and debated whether or not I should wait for him outside. I hadn't seen Lily in two weeks and she'd made it perfectly clear that she didn't want to see me. Her emails about being sick were obviously a ploy to get out of having to endure an awkward situation.

Julian knocked on their door, and I took a deep breath. My heart was racing from my bike ride. I'd pedaled fast and that's why it was hard to breathe. *That's why.*

Josephine pulled the door open and greeted us with a smile that faltered for only a moment when she saw me.

"Dean! I didn't realize you were with Julian."

Julian dipped down and gave her a kiss as we stepped through the front door.

"We were on a bike ride when you called," I explained, scanning the apartment for Lily. It was a tiny space and it only took a second to realize she wasn't there.

I hadn't considered the fact that she wouldn't be home

and I hated the ideas that cropped up in my head for why she wasn't there. Had she spent the night out somewhere? With the blind date guy?

I stepped farther into the apartment and caught sight of an enormous empty jar with my name on it on the countertop. Josephine caught my line of sight and bolted toward it, ripping it away before I could make out all of the words.

I smirked.

She cleared her throat and hid it as best as she could. "That was nothing. Just a...dumb game we were playing."

I opened my mouth to reassure her that I hadn't seen all of it as the front door opened behind us.

"Jo, I know I said I was going to run errands, but the bakery downstairs had a sale on croissants, so I had to stop and get some." The three of us turned toward the door to see Lily walk into the apartment clutching a brown bag full of croissants in her arms. "And then I couldn't keep walking around with a bag of croissants, right?" She dropped her keys in a little bowl by the door, dropped the bakery bag on the kitchen table, and then froze in place as her gaze met mine.

"What the ever-loving fuck are you doing here?" she asked, narrowing her eyes with a fierceness I hadn't seen in weeks. I forgot how quickly her claws could come out.

I laughed and then quickly stole back the sound. Laughing wouldn't make her less angry, even if she had just said something funny.

"He came with me—" Julian began, thinking he could throw me a lifeline.

"I came to help fix your dishwasher," I said, crossing my arms.

She shook her head. "We don't need your help."

I stared as she waltzed over to the dishwasher to prove her statement. She locked the door, pressed a few buttons, and then the dishwasher emitted a noise that sounded distinctly like metal scraping against metal. I cringed as it echoed around the apartment.

She smirked and shot me a glare. "It's *supposed* to make that noise."

She paused the cycle, opened the door, and pulled out a fork bent into three different directions. "*See?* It's clean."

I held back my smile. I missed her so much. This. The fiery woman who wasn't afraid to challenge me every step of the way. She infuriated me, but I'd trade it all to have one more fight with her, one more indignant glare from her bright brown eyes.

"Lily, do you want to, ah, come with me into the bathroom really quick?" Josephine asked with a clear strain to her voice.

Lily titled her head, trying to piece together what she meant.

Josephine cleared her throat and wrapped her hand around her neck, rubbing back and forth a few times. When I glanced back at Lily, her eyes were wide. Josephine's warning clicked for her at the same time I noticed a familiar ribbon hanging around her neck. It dipped down into her black tank top, tucked away so that I couldn't see the bottom. I didn't need to; I recognized the medal right away.

"How did you...?" I asked, stepping forward and reaching out for it.

Lily stepped back. "I went. I was there at the ceremony. Not for *you* specifically," she said, swallowing down her nerves and trying for a new approach. "I saw you leave the medal."

I smirked. "You were in the bathroom?"

She squeezed her eyes shut and shook her head. "No. It wasn't like that."

This was it, the only second chance I'd ever get. Lily still cared about me. She cared enough to wear my medal around her neck.

The medal and that ridiculous jar told me everything I needed to know.

It wasn't over.

CHAPTER FORTY-NINE

LILY

I WAS DOING my best to devour the entire bag of bargain croissants when Josephine set down two cups of coffee on our kitchen table.

"Did you check with the nunnery in Sweden to see if they had any openings?" I asked, shoving more of the flaky pastry into my mouth before I'd finished my question.

She studied me over her coffee cup. "You aren't religious."

"I could be, Jo. After this afternoon, I'm willing to try anything." I shook my head.

"It wasn't that bad."

HA.

I glared at her. "HE SAW THE JAR. He saw me wearing his medal like a freaking crazy person!"

"He didn't technically see the medal, only the ribbon…"

I dropped my head so that my forehead rested against

the edge of the table. "Jo. He ran out of this apartment so fast I thought there would be a Dean-shaped hole in the door."

She grimaced. "I'm not going to sugarcoat it. It was bad—*really* bad—but you still have a trillion guys in the city to date. Just because Dean thinks you're psycho doesn't mean every guy will."

"I don't want to date any other guys."

I don't want to date any other guys.

It hurt worse every time I repeated it in my head.

I wanted Dean.

I wanted the one man who now definitely wanted me locked up in a mental institution.

Lovely.

● ● ●

In a normal situation, I'd go through the stages of breakup grief and move on like I had from every other man in my life.

Stage One: Eat a bag of croissants. *Done.*

Stage Two: Try to land the role of next season's Bachelorette. *The producers never emailed me back.*

Stage Three: Consider, but don't actually make, a major life change…like a belly button ring or a tattoo. In the end, I parted my hair *slightly* more to the left.

All three stages were complete, it'd been three weeks since Dean had walked—no, *ran* out of my apartment, and I still couldn't stop thinking about him. I no longer wore his medal, but I did sleep with it under my pillow. I touched it every night before I went to sleep, just to confirm it was still there.

With a usual breakup, we'd part ways and stop seeing each other. With Dean, that wasn't possible. He was still my boss and I still had to see his name pop up in my email every morning. His messages always pertained to work and they always made my heart sink. I'd hold my breath, read through them, and then spend half an hour constructing a single sentence that I thought came off as equal parts bitchy and aloof.

Seeing him in person was the real danger, something I'd tried my hardest to avoid but could no longer put off.

He'd scheduled a meeting for early Monday morning. Zoe, Julian, and I were sitting in his office in the back of Provisions, waiting for him to arrive, and I swore my lungs weren't working.

"Is it hot in here to anyone else?" I asked, waving a hand in front of my face to get some airflow. Why was it so hard to breathe?

Zoe glanced over at me. "You're being weird."

"Am not."

Julian fired off an email he'd been typing on his phone and angled his body toward me. "You good, Lil?"

I didn't look him in the eye. I couldn't. It'd be like looking my dad in the eye when I was on the brink of tears. The floodgates would open whether I wanted them to or not.

"Peachy."

The A/C unit kicked on and I sighed with relief. At least I wouldn't be sweating buckets when Dean arrived.

"Jo said you might still be feeling sick," he offered.

We both knew sick was a euphemism and a poor one at that.

I shrugged. "I think I'll be *sick* for a while."

Zoe blanched. "What the hell do you have? Ebola?"

243

I laughed. "No." I began to clarify, and then Dean's office door opened so I paused.

He walked in...and I could hear my heart thumping in my ears...and I gripped the arm of my chair...and I inhaled his cologne. It'd been three weeks since I'd last smelled it and no department store sample could compare.

I knew I wouldn't last another day working for him. Working with Dean had been a dream come true, but now it felt like living through a nightmare. His intensity would never dull. His dark eyes would never lighten. His sharp mouth would never cease to amaze me. It'd been a foolish fight from the very beginning.

"Lily," he said.

I'd wanted so badly to fall in love with him. I'd wanted it so badly that I'd ignored the warning signs. I was the naive girl from Texas, swept up in a man who'd only ever thought of her as a stepping stone along the path to success.

"Lily," Julian said, shaking my hand on my chair.

I blinked and glanced toward him.

"Dean's trying to get your attention and you're completely zoned out," he said with a laugh. "Have we ruled Ebola out?"

I smiled halfheartedly and glanced at Dean, trying to guard my heart as best as I could. "Sorry about that."

His dark gaze held mine as he leaned over his desk. His mouth was pulled into a thin line. He was a statue of a man, unyielding at his core. "I just need you to hang back after the meeting for a few minutes. Is that okay?"

I nodded, not because I relished the idea of having alone time with him, but because it would give me the perfect chance to put in my two weeks notice.

CHAPTER FIFTY

DEAN

LILY CLOSED THE door behind Julian and Zoe, but she didn't turn to face me right away. We'd been there before, alone in my office. It was a recipe for disaster, and we both knew it. She rotated around to face me slowly, keeping hold of the doorknob behind her back like a lifeline. She rolled her lips together and I opened my mouth to speak first, but she beat me to the punch.

"I'd like to put in my two weeks notice."

I took a deep breath, processing her request.

She wants to leave?

I shook my head, just once.

"No."

Her eyes blazed with a new fury. "No?"

I glanced down and started to scroll through the calendar on my phone. I tried to focus on a specific date, but I kept scrolling through the months, right into the next year. "We need to plan a time to meet. The kitchen will be finished next week and I'm bringing Antonio out—"

"You're not listening to me," she argued, releasing the doorknob and stepping closer.

My gaze shot up to her and her eyes focused in, narrowing until I knew I had her undivided attention.

"Yes I am. I'm just ignoring you." I glanced back down at my phone. "I don't accept your resignation."

"What the hell—"

"Now, what day can you meet for the menu sampling? Monday?"

She paused on the other side of my desk and put her hand over my phone, blocking next year's calendar from my view.

"Dean. Let me go."

"No."

"*Fire me.*"

I shook my head and clenched my jaw to keep from saying something too soon.

She stepped back and threw her hands up in defeat. "What's the point of this? Do you really want me working for you still?"

"Yes. I do."

She put her face in her hands and shook it back and forth, so defeated.

What did she think? That I would let her walk away from me? After everything? She kept my goddamn medal around her neck and she was going to give up that easily?

"Monday at 5 PM, meet me at the building where Hunter was going to open Ivy & Wine."

She furrowed her brows, trying her hardest to keep her tears at bay. "Please don't make me."

Two taps sounded on the closed door and a moment later, Zoe's head popped through the gap. "Boss-man, the

Provisions staff meeting starts in ten." Her gaze shifted from me to Lily, and then her smile faded. "Should I postpone it?"

I shook my head and rounded the desk, pausing as my shoulder brushed against Lily's. "If you still want to quit after Monday, then I'll respect your decision."

Her fiery brown eyes turned to me. Her lips were the closest they'd been in weeks, red and swollen from her rubbing them together. It was painful to keep my distance, but I wouldn't win her back with a half-baked speech in my office. She deserved more, and I was prepared to give her everything I had.

"I'm not coming," she said, so softly that Zoe couldn't hear.

I bent toward her, brushing my hand against hers and squeezing once before letting go.

"Please."

CHAPTER FIFTY-ONE

LILY

I SPENT THE remainder of the week getting my ducks in a row. Dean would need to replace me and I didn't want to make it harder on him than it had to be. Everything I was working on—seasonal cocktail menus, wine lists, menu ideas, and potential pairings—was now neatly typed up and saved to a thumb drive. I wasn't nearly finished with any of it, but I tried to condense my ideas as sensibly as possible so that his next consultant could pick up right where I left off.

I had no clue what I would do for work. I would have loved to find another consulting job, but I knew it wouldn't be possible without more experience. I could have asked Dean for a letter of recommendation, but I was too prideful. I'd scrimp and save and focus my energy on my blog for a little bit. If web traffic to my reviews started taking off, that would generate a little bit of income, and in the meantime, there was always bartending. It wasn't stimulating work, but the tips would help sustain me until I figured out what I would do.

"So what are you doing tonight?" Josephine asked as she came out of the bathroom decked out in a killer dress. The smooth material was breezy and swayed side to side as she walked toward the kitchen table. She reached for a pair of dangling earrings, sliding the first one in as she assessed me on the futon.

I held up my laptop. "Working."

She arched a dark brow and then nodded. "On restaurant reviews?"

I nodded, glancing back down at the blinking curser on my laptop. I'd started typing a sentence thirty minutes ago and had yet to finish.

La Patisserie is…

Is what?

A good restaurant?

A bad restaurant?

Apparently, I couldn't even get that far.

"It's going really well," I lied.

She nodded, indulging me.

"So you aren't going?"

She didn't even need to clarify where. The night before, she'd talked my ear off about why I should give Dean another chance. I didn't agree. Dean and I weren't a couple. I'd worn my heart on my sleeve and I'd gotten burned. End of story. No epilogue, no encore, no second chances.

"I love you, but I think you're making a huge mistake," she said, tucking her clutch under her arm.

I let my head fall back against the futon.

"You look really pretty."

She rolled her eyes, annoyed with me for ignoring her protests. It wouldn't do any good for her to keep badgering me. The more she told me to go, the more I wanted to stay.

"It doesn't matter anyway. It's already 7 PM. He's not there any more."

"So you stood him up?" she asked, a sour expression marring her pretty features.

"Don't make it more dramatic than it is, Jo."

She shook her head, but I could see the sadness there. I could tell she wanted to ask me more, to push me to fight for him, but she stayed quiet as she packed up her clutch. She was heading for the door, off to meet Julian for a date, when I realized something.

"You know, Jo, I always thought I wanted a relationship like you and Julian's, but I don't. I don't want it to be that easy. I hated Dean just as much as I loved him. How twisted is that?"

She pressed her lips together and her sad gaze hit the floor before she glanced back at me. "In the beginning, I thought you two would tear each other apart."

I stared at where his medal sat on our coffee table. It was always near me, always reminding me of what I'd almost had.

"I guess I wasn't that far off."

I never replied and she left for her date. The door closed, leaving me in silence, and I settled back on the futon. There was no point in second-guessing my decision. I hadn't lied to Josephine. Dean had asked me to meet him two hours earlier, I'd stood him up, and that was that.

I picked up a magazine and covered his medal, tucking the ribbon underneath so that it was completely out of sight. I grabbed my laptop and pulled up my favorite restaurant blog. It was useless to try and force myself to work. I just wanted to distract myself until I was tired enough to sleep.

The blog, New In New York, highlighted up-and-coming restaurants, breaking foodie news before anyone else. Usually, the posts interested me, but I was nearly halfway down the front page before a post caught my eye. More specifically, a photo caught my eye. It was a street view image of the building Dean had purchased from Hunter. The construction was further along, but it was definitely the same place.

I scrolled back to the top of the post and started from the beginning.

Manhattan's Finest Set to Open Lirio

Fresh on the heels of winning the James Beard Award for Outstanding Restaurateur, Dean Harper is set to open his new restaurant, Lirio, next month. We haven't been able to pin down details on the menu yet, but with a name like that, one can only hope it will have a Spanish flare. Tapas and margaritas anyone?

We managed to snap this photo of the outside of the restaurant, but the windows are taped up during the interior construction phase. Sneaky sneaky. As soon as we have more details, we'll be sure to pass them along!

Also, to save you the Google search, Lirio translated into English means Lily. Dean Harper is a notorious bachelor, so we have no clue where the name came from. His grandmother? A friend? PLEASE DON'T SAY IT'S HIS GIRLFR—

I started the article again, this time reading each word as

slowly as possible. Dean was opening a restaurant and he was naming it after me. He was naming his restaurant after me and I'd stood him up.

I slapped my laptop closed and tossed it onto the futon. I turned in a circle, trying to think of what to do first. I was wearing a t-shirt and no bra. Shit. I threw off my pajamas and rifled through my closet, trying to find a single clean shirt. I hadn't had the energy to do laundry in days. I grabbed a black sundress and yanked it on over my head, then yanked it off and put on a bra.

I had my keys in hand and my purse over my shoulder when I flew through the front door. It wasn't until I was halfway down the stairs that I realized I wasn't wearing any shoes.

"SHIT!" I yelled, turning and running back toward my apartment.

This was the closest Dean would ever come to commitment, and I had no shoes. I needed to find him. I needed to apologize for standing him up and I needed to find some freaking shoes!

It was already 7:30 PM. Dean definitely wasn't still at the restaurant, so I took off in the direction of his house. I didn't want to wait for a cab, so I hoofed it on foot, my flip-flops slapping against the concrete as I made a run for it. I turned the corner and took off down the sidewalk, nearly plowing down a girl Instagramming her ice cream cone.

"Watch it!" she spat as I brushed past her.

"No, YOU watch it," I yelled back. I wasn't taking anyone's shit. I had to get across town and I couldn't waste a single second.

Flip-flops were a terrible choice of footwear for a cross-Manhattan run. I knew I'd be nursing blisters for the next two years.

"Oh god, I'm not going to make it," I hissed, leaning against a brick wall and trying to catch my breath.

I was almost there, but my heart was going to give out if I kept running. I turned to the side and caught sight of my reflection in the window of the building. *Holy shit.* Not good.

I hadn't put makeup on that morning *or* washed my hair the night before. Not that it really mattered; most of the blonde strands were sticky with sweat and stuck to my forehead in a grungy sort of look. My cheeks were flushed, and my eyes were wide—that may sound cute, but it wasn't. My black dress was stuck to my chest with sweat, but thankfully the dark color sort of concealed my general lack of hygiene.

I forced myself to ignore my appearance and kept going. I pushed off the wall and took a deep breath. Dean's house was only a few blocks away.

I'm almost there.

CHAPTER FIFTY-TWO

LILY

I RANG THE doorbell twice and then knocked with my fist. The light turned on in the foyer and then his black lacquered door slid open. He stood on the other side, shirtless and silhouetted by the light behind him. His black drawstrings pants were untied and loose around his hips—clearly he didn't know proper protocol for how to answer a door.

"You're too late," he said, careful to keep the emotion out of his voice.

I took a step back before meeting his gaze. I'd seen him angry before, on *multiple* occasions, but I'd never seen him defeated. His eyes were soft, his lips were downturned, and his brows were furrowed not in anger, but in pain.

"You named it after me," I said, barely above a whisper.

He swallowed slowly and then nodded. "And every single dish was inspired by you, and every wine tastes like you, and every painting hung on the walls was commissioned in your honor."

"Dean—"

"Too bad you missed it."

"Show me," I pleaded.

He took a step back. "I think I'm good."

"Dean. *Show me*."

He laughed, but it was a hollow sound, something I never wanted to hear again. "Antonio is gone. The food is in the restaurant's kitchen, cold and forgotten."

He moved to close the door, but I put my hand out to block its path. If he closed it, he'd chop my hand off. I wouldn't put it past him, but I had to at least try to stop him.

"Dean. *Please* take me to Lirio."

A tiny spark lit up behind his sad eyes. "I waited there for two hours. I sat in the restaurant by myself, waiting for the door to open. You never showed up and it's too late to go back now."

I could visualize him there perfectly, that glimmer of hope in his eyes. He'd thought I'd show. What had it felt like to put the food away in the fridge after waiting there alone for two hours? I wanted to wrap my arms around him and make it up to him, but I knew he would pull away. We didn't work like normal people. We were stubborn and proud.

I knew I had to work for his forgiveness, so I took a step back and then felt for the hand railing on his stoop. I used it to guide me down the steps backward. All the while, he stood in his doorway, on the precipice of shutting me out of his life for good.

I kept walking backward, keeping my eyes on him until I was in the middle of the sidewalk. Then, I flung my arms out to my side and yelled at the top of my lungs, "I'm sorry! I'm SORRY! DO YOU HEAR ME NEW YORK

CITY?!" I twisted around in a circle and yelled out to the houses around me.

"I stood up a wonderful man and I'M SORRRRYYYYYY!"

A car alarm went off a few streets over and I swore I heard a cat screech with annoyance down the block.

I stopped twirling and dropped my hands back to my sides, facing Dean with absolute abandon.

"I'm sorry," I said, one last time, just for him. It was sincere and real and it was the best I could do.

We stood frozen, staring at one another. He kept his position in the doorway and I stayed outside, giving him space. I thought he'd turn and walk. After everything we'd put each other through, the odds of him loving me the way I loved him weren't in my favor.

"Please," I said, trying to convince him.

He inhaled a deep breath, shook his head, and then he held up a finger. "Lirio's closed, but luckily, I know the owner."

● ● ●

We didn't speak the entire walk to the restaurant, and we tried our hardest not to look at one another. Every so often, I felt his eyes on me and I'd turn to face him. He'd glance away and I'd be left with a view of his profile, so achingly beautiful that I couldn't help but stare for a moment. Halfway there, I couldn't stand it any longer. "I see you watching me," he said.

"I see you watching me," he said.

"Look, I know we're still testing the waters here, and you're doing me a big favor by agreeing to go with me, but…I ran all the way to your apartment in mismatched flip-flops and my feet are basically two giant blisters right now. Would you mind giving me a piggyback ride?"

He laughed and turned so I could hop onto his back. My feet thanked me the second I was off the ground.

"Better?" he asked.

I smiled. "Much."

His grip tightened around my thighs and he carried me until we reached the restaurant.

The photo on the blog must have been recent because the windows of the restaurant were still taped up and the facade still lacked its finishing touches. The brick was painted black and the building was dark, but the streetlights illuminated a thin plastic banner hanging just above the door. Lirio was spelled across it in black scrolling letters.

"It's beautiful," I said, sliding my gaze to him.

He brushed off my compliment. "It's not done yet."

"Well, I love it already."

His smile hit me full force when he turned to me. "Me too."

"Did you taste the food earlier? When Antonio was here?"

He shook his head.

"Come on. Let's heat it up and try it."

"It won't be nearly as good," he said.

It was.

Of course Antonio would have plated the food with pretty details, but we managed just fine. The dishes were delicious, full of complex flavors that I had to sit and mull over as I chewed each bite. Dean and I fought each other for each morsel until the very end and even then, I still wanted more.

"Here," he said, holding out his fork with the last bite of

257

our dessert resting on top.

I smile and leaned forward, letting him feed me. The cheesecake tart with fresh blueberries was the perfect ending to the meal. The creamy texture rolled over my tongue and I let a soft moan escape my mouth.

"It's exactly what I wanted," I said, waving my hand over the empty plates and bowls. "This is the kind of meal I was expecting in Vegas."

He nodded, watching me over the kitchen island.

"I'm sorry I didn't come earlier," I said, broaching the subject I'd avoided throughout dinner.

He dropped his fork onto his empty plate and met my gaze. "A part of me knew you wouldn't show up."

"Why?"

"Because if someone had treated me the way I'd treated you, I wouldn't have given them another chance either."

"Is that what you wanted? A second chance?"

He wet his bottom lip and for a few seconds, I wasn't sure he'd even answer.

"Dean?"

"The other day you said that no man is an island. Ever since I was young, I've been fiercely competitive. I guess I always thought of myself as a mountain climber. I wanted to be the fastest kid on the track, the smartest kid in the class, and the richest man in New York. I wanted to climb and climb and climb, but the top turned out to be an even colder type of isolation."

"Are you saying you need a Sherpa?"

He laughed and bent forward over the island to kiss me. He took me by surprise and I could hardly kiss him back before he was pulling away.

"I need *you*," he confirmed. "God help me."

I smiled, flushed from ear to ear with a blush I didn't

bother trying to hide.

"When I pushed you out of my house that night, I told you that you'd find a better man than me, and well, I've decided that *I'm* going to be that man. In the last month, I've worked to become the type of man you deserve."

"Oh really?" I asked, trying to keep my cool. Inside, I was pushing down the urge to shove the dishes off the island and throw myself at him.

"I sold off four of my restaurants, I hired three new managers to help with the workload, and I promoted Zoe so that she can help with daily operations. I won't ever fully retire, but I'm not going to be a workaholic any more."

"What about Lirio? You didn't sell it, right?"

I'd kill him if he had.

He shook his head. "I still own Lirio. It'll always be our restaurant."

I smiled and leaned in, whispering against his lips just before I kissed him.

"The first of many."

EPILOGUE

DEAN

I RECLINED ON the back seat of the town car and let the city lights ease my growing headache. My flight from Iowa had landed an hour ahead of schedule, but the traffic from the airport to Lirio was about to drive me insane..

The driver's voice broke me out of my haze. "How was your trip, sir?"

I turned toward the front seat and met his eye in the rearview mirror. "The usual."

My parents had badgered me the same as they always had, but this time Lily had been the topic of discussion.

"When are we going to get a grandchild? We're only getting older."

"Are you sure you want to stay in New York City? Is that really where you want to raise your family?"

"Aren't you ready to make an honest woman out of her?"

I swore they were still living in the 1800s, but I'd tried

my best to appease them. I'd had a ring burning a hole in the pocket of my pants for the last two months. I'd picked out a ring that was big, but tasteful. Julian had set the bar high a few months earlier—*the bastard*—but I'd been happy to spoil Lily. She'd flip when she saw it. *If* she saw it.

Our lives had been so busy the last few months. Opening Lirio had taken a lot of work and the restaurant still wasn't running smoothly. Most nights, Lily and I were both working like dogs.

"Here you are sir. Would you like me to wait?"

I shook my head and offered him a tip. The night was still young and I knew Lily and I would be at the restaurant for quite a while.

"Go on ahead and drop my luggage at the house. We'll catch a cab later."

"Sounds good, sir."

Lirio was packed when I walked in, busier than usual for a Wednesday night. The New York Times had featured our restaurant the week before and we were already starting to see the effects of the article.

"Hi Mr. Harper," the hostess said, nodding at me as I walked in and hung my jacket on the coat rack near the door.

"Hey Sarah. What's it looking like tonight?"

"We have over a hundred reservations and I haven't tallied the walk-ins yet. There are two parties taking place in the back rooms at the moment."

I nodded. "Good. Where's Lily?"

She smiled and angled her head toward the center bar.

"Again?"

"Yeah, Todd called in sick."

That was fourth time he'd called in sick in two weeks,

and I knew for a fact the kid was calling in so he could make it to last minute auditions.

"All right, thanks," I told her, moving past the hostess stand so I could find Lily.

We'd designed Lirio to be much smaller than Provisions. We'd wanted the experience to feel intimate. The tables were covered with white tablecloths with fresh flowers and tea candles. The lighting overhead was soft and meant to be forgotten. Beautiful abstract paintings hung sparingly on the walls, but the real art was the food. Antonio had created dishes for us that were jam-packed with color and flavor.

"Two jalapeño margaritas!" Lily called, sliding two drinks across the bar. There was a small crowd around her, watching her work and waiting anxiously for their turn to get a drink.

There was another bar on the other side of the restaurant, but like always, people were drawn to her. She had her blonde hair twisted up in a bun atop her head, but a few strands had slipped out. She huffed out a breath, trying to blow the strands out of her eyes as she dried her hands on her black apron. She wasn't in the standard black uniform the other employees wore; she never was. Just like the food, she was a constant source of color in the restaurant. Her royal blue wrap dress curved around her, completely modest but lighting a fire inside me even still. She was beautiful. Hours of working behind a bar would never dampen her glow.

I walked up to the edge of the bar, a few feet away from where she was stationed. She bent forward toward a patron to hear his order over the hum of the crowd. When she leaned back and reached for her shaker, I spoke up.

"You told me you were going to catch up on admin

stuff tonight," I said.

Her bright eyes slid from the shaker up to me and she squealed.

"Dean!"

She took two steps closer and leaned over the bar to plant a kiss right on my lips. I wrapped a hand around her neck, holding her against me.

"I missed you," I breathed against her lips.

"I need to make this drink," she laughed, peeling out of my hold.

I regretted having to let her go, but there were customers waiting for drinks.

"You want me to help?" I asked.

There'd been a few nights in the last month when Lily and I'd had to tackle bar duty together.

She scooped some ice into the shaker and shook her head. "Nah, there's plenty to do in the office and I don't want to be here until 3 AM again."

Her mischievous smile confirmed that she was referring to the week before when we'd worked late and shared Chinese food in the back office. She'd leaned over to wipe something from the edge of my mouth, I'd licked her finger, and we'd ended up on the floor in a messy pile of love and lo mein.

I tapped my knuckle against the bar. "Come find me when it slows down."

● ● ●

There was a knock on the office door and I glanced up as Lily strolled in, kicking the door shut behind her. She held a bottle of chilled champagne in one hand and two champagne glasses in the other.

"How were your parents?" she asked.

I leaned back in my chair and motioned her forward.

"Good, but they were sad you couldn't make it. Why the champagne?"

She slid down onto my lap and I wrapped my hands around her waist. She nuzzled the side of my neck and I inhaled her sweet perfume.

"It's to celebrate."

"Celebrate what?" I asked, pulling back so I could look into her eyes.

She smiled. "This place has been open for almost six months. That article in the Times has taken our business to a new level. I think we have like two-hundred and fifty reservations for Friday night already."

I drew a strand of hair off her cheek. "Are you happy with it? The hours and the work?"

She shot me a sidelong glance. "Are you kidding me?"

The Times article had been a human interest piece more than a food critique. Word got out soon after we opened that I'd opened the restaurant in Lily's honor. The dishes and their names were all charmingly named for her. She'd become something of a celebrity in the food world overnight, but there was no time to relish in the popularity except for stolen moments in our back office with stolen champagne.

"What about you?" she asked.

"I'm happy if you're happy."

She rolled her eyes at my cheesy comment and then held up the champagne. "Should I pop it open?"

"I have something to ask you first," I said, feeling the weight of the ring in my pocket.

She rubbed her lips together to contain her grin. "I think

I already know what it is."

"Do you?"

She nodded. "I found something in your pants the other week when I was doing laundry."

"Lily—"

She smiled and kissed me.

"And guess what?" she continued.

"What?"

"I already tried it on."

I shook my head, surprised that she'd been able to keep the secret as long as she had.

"Did you?"

She nodded, not the least bit ashamed. "And I might have also sent a photo of it to Jo."

I laughed. I shouldn't have been surprised. This was Lily after all. "Well then I guess I don't even have to ask you then?"

Her eyes widened with the fire I'd grown to love. "You'd better ask me, Dean Harper."

I shrugged, trying to play it off. "Nah. I think I'll wait for a better moment. Maybe I'll plan something next month? Or maybe next spring when the trees look nice in Central Park?"

She fumed at the idea of waiting that long. "Please don't make me wait."

I shook my head. "This can't be our story. We can't get engaged in the back of our restaurant."

Her head fell to my chest and she rocked it back and forth. "No! I want this story. *This*, right here."

I already had the ring in the palm of my hand. There was no way I'd wait another minute.

"Lily Noelle Black."

She smiled and I could feel her body shake with

excitement.

"Would you do me the honor…"

Her big eyes stared up at me with unabashed expectation.

"…of opening that champagne? I'm parched from my plane ride."

"DEAN!"

She slapped my chest and tried to move off my lap. I'd teased her too much and she wasn't going to let me get away with it. Too bad for her, I already had her hand in mine and the ring was poised at the end of her finger, ready to rest in its rightful place.

"Marry me, Lily. Marry me. There's no one in the world better suited than the two of us. I can't promise that we won't fight—you know I'd be lying if I did—but I promise that no one will ever love you more than I do."

She laughed and nodded over and over again as I slid the ring onto her finger.

"You're going to drive me insane, I already know it," she said.

I smiled.

"You know…most people just say yes."

She narrowed her eyes and slipped her hands to either side of my cheeks. I knew she was about to kiss me and I inhaled just before her lips brushed mine.

"Yeah well, *we aren't most people*."

THE END

The Allure of Dean Harper

R.S. Grey

ACKNOWLEDGEMENTS

This book is for my loyal readers. Over the last two years, your love and support for my books has completely changed my life. I cannot thank you enough!

All my love,
Rachel

OTHER BOOKS BY R.S.GREY:

READ ABOUT JOSEPHINE AND JULIAN'S LOVE STORY IN:
THE ALLURE OF JULIAN LEFRAY
ADULT ROMANCE

From: JosephineKeller@LLDesigns.com
To: LilyNBlack@gmail.com
Subject: Justin Timberlake Nudes!

Lily, you predictable perv. I knew you'd open this email faster if I tempted you with a glimpse of JT's "PP". Well, put your pants back on and grab some bubbly because I have much better news to share.

I GOT A JOB!

As of tomorrow, I'll be the new executive assistant at Lorena Lefray Designs. I am SO excited, but there's one itty bitty problem: I won't be Lorena's assistant. I'll be working for her older brother, Julian.

I know what you're thinking- *"But Jo, what's the problem?"*

Google him. *Now.* He's the man in the fitted navy suit whose face reminds you that there's hope yet for this cruel, ugly world. Keep scrolling...Do you see those dimples? *Yup.* That's the Julian Lefray I will be reporting to tomorrow morning.

Lord, help us all...

XO,
Jo

SCORING WILDER
USA TODAY BESTSELLER
NEW ADULT SPORTS ROMANCE

What started out as a joke--seduce Coach Wilder--soon became a goal she had to score.

With Olympic tryouts on the horizon, the last thing nineteen-year-old Kinsley Bryant needs to add to her plate is Liam Wilder. He's a professional soccer player, America's favorite bad-boy, and has all the qualities of a skilled panty-dropper.

* A face that makes girls weep - check.

* Abs that can shred Parmesan cheese (the expensive kind) - check.

* Enough confidence to shift the earth's gravitational pull - double check.

Not to mention Liam is strictly off limits. Forbidden. Her coaches have made that perfectly clear. (i.e. "Score with Coach Wilder anywhere other than the field and you'll be cut from the team faster than you can count his tattoos.") But that just makes him all the more enticing...Besides, Kinsley's already counted the visible ones, and she is not one to leave a project unfinished.

Kinsley tries to play the game her way as they navigate through forbidden territory, but Liam is determined to teach her a whole new definition for the term "team bonding."

THE DUET
ADULT ROMANCE

When 27-year-old pop sensation Brooklyn Heart steps in front of a microphone, her love songs enchant audiences worldwide. But when it comes to her own love life, the only spell she's under is a dry one.

So when her label slots her for a Grammy performance with the sexy and soulful Jason Monroe, she can't help but entertain certain fantasies... those in which her G-string gets more play than her guitars'.

Only one problem. Jason is a lyrical lone wolf that isn't happy about sharing the stage—nor his ranch — with the sassy singer. But while it may seem like a song entitled 'Jason Monroe Is an Arrogant Ho' basically writes itself, their label and their millions of fans are expecting recording gold...

They're expecting *The Duet.*

THE DESIGN
ADULT ROMANCE

Five minutes until the interview begins.

Fresh on the heels of her college graduation, Cameron Heart has landed an interview at a prestigious architecture firm.

Four minutes until the interview.

She knows she's only there because the owner, Grayson Cole, is her older sister's friend.

Three minutes.

For the last seven years, Grayson has been the most intimidating man Cammie has ever had the pleasure, or *displeasure*, of being around.

Two Minutes.

But the job opportunity is too good to pass up. So, Cammie will have to ignore the fact that Grayson is handsome enough to have his own national holiday.

One.

After all, she shouldn't feel that way about her new boss. And, he *will* be her new boss.

...

"I'm not intimidated by you," I said with a confident smile. "Perhaps we should fix that, Ms. Heart. Close the door."

273

R.S. Grey

WITH THIS HEART
NEW ADULT ROMANCE

If someone had told me a year ago that I was about to fall in love, go on an epic road trip, ride a Triceratops, sing on a bar, and lose my virginity, I would have assumed they were on drugs.

Well, that is, until I met Beckham.

Beck was mostly to blame for my recklessness. Gorgeous, clever, undeniably charming Beck barreled into my life as if it were his mission to make sure I never took living for granted. He showed me that there were no boundaries, rules were for the spineless, and a kiss was supposed to happen when I least expected.

Beck was the plot twist that took me by surprise. Two months before I met him, death was knocking at my door. I'd all but given up my last scrap of hope when suddenly I was given a second chance at life. This time around, I wasn't going to let it slip through my fingers.

We set out on a road trip with nothing to lose and no guarantees of tomorrow.

Our road trip was about young, reckless love. The kind of love that burns bright.

The kind of love that no road-map could bring me back from.

BEHIND HIS LENS
ADULT ROMANCE

Twenty-three year old model Charley Whitlock built a quiet life for herself after disaster struck four years ago. She hides beneath her beautiful mask, never revealing her true self to the world... until she comes face-to-face with her new photographer — sexy, possessive Jude Anderson. It's clear from the first time she meets him that she's playing by his rules. He says jump, she asks how high. He tells her to unzip her cream Dior gown, she knows she has to comply. But what if she wants him to take charge outside of the studio as well?

Jude Anderson has a strict "no model" dating policy. But everything about Charley sets his body on fire.

When a tropical photo shoot in Hawaii forces the stubborn pair into sexually charged situations, their chemistry can no longer be ignored. They'll have to decide if they're willing to break their rules and leave the past behind or if they'll stay consumed by their demons forever. Will Jude persuade Charley to give in to her deepest desires?